More Tales from my
Welsh Village

Amazon reviews for
Tales from my Welsh Village

★ ★ ★ ★ ★

Tales from my Welsh Village cleverly marries humour with nostalgia to give a realistic representation of working-class village life in the Sixties. It is a triumph. – *Happy reader*

★ ★ ★ ★ ★

Tales from My Welsh Village is exactly that: stories based on what one hears, sees, and experiences while growing up in a small Welsh town. These Welsh tales become every reader's tales, and they're funny and poignant, and nostalgic, and most of all true. – *Glynn Young*

★ ★ ★ ★ ★

Very funny tale of Welsh mischief. The characters really come to life as you lose yourself in the stories… It reminded me of my formative years in my local pub, when the pub was the centre of the community and inhabited by similar villains to the crew of the Plough Inn. Read it and enjoy. – *The bookworm*

★ ★ ★ ★ ★

I so enjoyed this novel – it paints such a vivid picture of working-class life in a small village in rural Wales in the '60s that you really feel like you've lived there too. A wonderful book. – *BwrwGlaw*

★ ★ ★ ★ ★

Brilliant. I couldn't put it down!! This book is fantastically written, and you can really imagine the characters as if you had known them all your lives. A worthy read! – *Kelster86*

More Tales from my Welsh Village

KEN SMITH

This book is dedicated to the memory of Trefor Plough,
Fred and Colin Howells (the 'Partners')
and all the other local characters who inspired this story.

First impression: 2021
© Ken Smith & Y Lolfa Cyf., 2021

Cover design: Y Lolfa and Ken Smith
Cover illustration: ᴍᴜᴍᴘʰ

ISBN: 978 1 78461 826 1

Published and printed in Wales
on paper from well-maintained forests by
Y Lolfa Cyf., Talybont, Ceredigion SY24 5HE
e-mail ylolfa@ylolfa.com
website www.ylolfa.com
tel 01970 832 304
fax 832 782

Prologue

RECENTLY I HAD an email from old friend from my youth and she told me this funny story...

The mobile librarian had been to her house the day before with her usual three books in the genre she liked. She said he had looked totally dejected. Naturally, she had asked him if he was unwell because he had looked so down in the mouth.

He told her no, he was okay, but for some reason he had not been able to exchange any books at all that week for any of his regular book customers.

She then asked him if he knew of any particular reason for this lack of support.

'Well,' he said, 'I have been asking at every house and it seems that everybody is too busy reading a book by some local author called Ken Smith who's now living in Canada.'

She told me he sounded so sad that she felt sorry for the poor dab. Can you imagine, after all these years of giving excellent service to the people in Rhyd-y-Groes, only to be told that this week they were too busy reading about some of the local characters who used to live in the village.

This book that all the locals were reading was my first book of reminiscences about Fred, Colin, Trefor and the crew at the Plough in Rhigos – Rhyd-y-groes – my old village. I've been over the moon since to hear how much people enjoyed that first book, and as I still had a wealth of other anecdotes about the ridiculous things they all got up to, I decided to write this second volume of stories of the old days. A lot of the tales here are loosely based on their real-life exploits, though others are fictional. And if you're not familiar with the way folk speak in Rhyd-y-groes, don't worry – there's a glossary at the back of the book.

I would like to take this opportunity to thank my everloving wife Avril for her tremendous support throughout my scribbling, Lefi Gruffudd and Carolyn Hodges for having confidence in me as a writer and everyone else at Y Lolfa for getting the publications to market, and last but not least, thanks to Mumph for his brilliant cover: for this I will be forever grateful.

Ken Smith
October 2021

CHAPTER 1

Colin in The Bird in Hand

THE MAIN BAR in the Plough Inn was fairly crowded, as usual on a Friday night, when parish councillors Johnny Wills and Alan George eased their way between the tables. Alan, leading the way, managed to find seats at the large farmhouse table, where the inevitable game of four-handed cribbage was taking place. Cribbage – or crib – is a card game for two teams of two people, invented in the early 1600s but as popular in pubs in the Sixties and Seventies as it was then. Alan and Johnny sat on opposite sides and Alan immediately rapped twice on Roy's homemade scoreboard to signify that he and his playing partner and brother-in-law, Johnny, were ready to challenge the winners of the current game for a pint a corner.

Colin Howells, eldest son of the late Fred Howells (whose life and escapades were an open book to everyone in the Plough and beyond), was in the midst of dealing the cards for the next hand when Alan sat down beside him and leaned heavily against him to announce his presence. Colin, feeling the pressure against his shoulder, looked to his right and found Alan's smiling face just inches away.

He grinned and said, 'Hello, Al. I thought it was you. I could smell that fancy aftershave you use to charm the knickers off those floosies all over the place.'

Alan laughed. 'Well, it seems to work most of the time, Col. How are things going with you, then? Have you moved back to the village? I'm only asking cos I've seen you about the place a lot and I can't imagine you driving back and forth to the Plough from Waun-gron when you've had a few drinks. Are you back in the village, then?'

Dealing the cards for the next hand, Colin replied, 'In the first place, Al, I don't have a bluddy car now. The bluddy finance company took it back because I couldn't keep up the payments.' He went on, 'After my father and me moved back to Waun-gron, he managed to wangle himself a flat in The Shelter. He was a bluddy good talker, mind. Well, I made friends with my mother and stayed with her, temporary like. Later, after my father died, I stayed on for a while with my mother until she got fed up with me not workin' regular. We ended up havin' a big row so in the end I left there. Lucky for me, my butty in work, Bobby Thomas – not 'im,' he said, indicating Bobby Price, his playing partner, 'Bobby's got a flat down by the chapel. He said he had a spare room I could use until I got sorted out. Kind of 'im, mind!'

Alan nodded his understanding of the situation, then asked, 'Are you working regular now?

'Not really,' Colin replied with a wry grin. 'Sometimes I think of my butty who crossed shifts with me and got in an accident underground and died from it. I get a bit worried about going down there. I'm okay if I'm working near the surface but... Aye, he got flattened by a runaway dram that came off the rails right by the parting. They got 'im to the hospital quick enough but when he died a few days later, the inquest said he'd died of a bad heart and not the accident. Bluddy NCB, anything to get out of payin' people compensation.'

He turned towards Alan and, lowering his voice, said quietly, 'See Al, I'm not *afraid* to work underground but I don't feel comfortable down there any more, and I'm always listenin' for something, instead of keepin' my mind on what I'm doin', and that's when accidents can happen.'

Alan nodded, and said quietly, 'I know exactly what you mean, Col. When I was working underground in the Tower – that was years and years ago, mind – I saw an accident with runaway drams and that made me think. So I found another job and ended up as a foreman on a job site and never looked back. Besides, the money was a lot better and I came home from work much cleaner too.' Together, the two men laughed about it.

'Fifteen two only,' Bobby called out his score.

'I've only got two pairs,' said Colin, 'but we're a street in front of these boys so it looks like you'll be playin' us next, Al. So, where are you two off to tonight, all dressed up?'

'We're going down to Neath, to the Bird in Hand. We yerd there's a good singsong there on Friday nights. We'll play the next game and have a pint, then we'll leave. Do you want to come with us?

'I'm still in my workin' clothes, mun.'

'That doesn't matter, Col. Who's going to notice in a crowd?' Johnny chipped in from across the table. 'C'mon, Col. It will be a jaunt out and will make a bit of a change from yere.' The Bird in Hand had been a pub in Neath for probably hundreds of years, and had been a meeting place for drovers and farmers to talk and exchange stories about their families and friends when the annual market convened.

'Aye okay, I'll come with you. I'll 'ave another pint while we play. Trefor! A pint of best, please.'

'Let me see your money first!' Trefor pretended to speak in stern tones, at the same time winking broadly at Roy, standing waiting patiently for his fresh pint to be pulled.

'I'll get that, Tref,' Alan called from the card table. 'And I'll have a bottle of brown ale to top up this pint. Do you want anything, Johnny?'

Johnny, shuffling the worn deck of cards, shook his head and began to deal the four hands.

Ten minutes later the game was over and Alan and Johnny rose from the table victorious, instructing the losers to put their winning pints over the bar for later.

Outside in the fresh air they walked towards Alan's Jaguar saloon, parked under the street light. Colin grinned and said in a high-pitched voice, 'There's posh, Alan!'

Alan looked over his shoulder. 'It's just a car, Colin. I didn't buy it new. It's nice to drive though. C'mon boys, let's get going or we'll be too late to get a seat.'

Arriving in Neath not ten minutes later, they made their way along Water Street and entered the crowded pub. They quickly found the singing room by following the noise of the piano. Johnny led the way across the room to an empty table close to the piano.

The pianist, whose name was Vic, had a terrible squint which reminded Johnny of Ben Turpin, the 1920s comedy film star. It was some time later, when they had had a few pints, that Johnny made the fatal mistake of mentioning this likeness to Colin.

Colin turned around to look directly at Vic and asked in a loud voice, 'Hey, Vic! Are you talking to me and looking at him, or looking at him and talking to me?'

The room went silent and Johnny and Alan immediately stood up with their backs to the wall. Being strangers in the pub, it was only natural for the locals to look out for one of their own.

Colin seemed oblivious to the situation he had created and was still sitting grinning at the pianist.

Vic looked around the room – as best he could – then started laughing and continued playing.

Immediately the noise in the room started up again as if nothing had happened.

Johnny and Alan slowly sat back down, with Johnny pretending to wipe the sweat from his brow, at the same time shaking his head in Colin's direction.

About an hour later Alan suggested that they go and get something to eat at the nearby Chinese restaurant, just off Windsor Road.

Colin shook his head. 'I've got no money for food, boys.'

'Don't worry about that, Col. It's my turn to buy,' Alan grinned. 'We need to have something to eat before driving back up the valley, just to sober up a bit.'

Entering the Bamboo Palace, they sat near the front window and waited patiently for their order to be taken, but it didn't appear as if anyone was serving in that area. It was only by chance that Colin started to whistle tunelessly. Suddenly there were three waiters at the side of the table, advising them, 'No whistle. Very bad luck!'

They each ordered a plate of prawns and fried rice, which appeared in front of them like magic.

'That's service for you,' said Colin with a broad grin. 'We'll 'ave to remember to whistle next time we come yere. Right, boys?'

Minutes later their plates were empty and the bill appeared the second they put their forks down. 'I think they want us out of yere pretty quick,' Johnny remarked. 'P'raps they think we're bad luck or something. You know how superstitious some people can be. C'mon, Col, let's get out of yere – Alan will look after the bill.'

As they approached the front door, a crowd of Chinese from the kitchen area surrounded them, all shouting at the same time. Then the manager appeared and accused them of trying to leave without paying. Johnny and Colin were rapidly getting annoyed when Alan appeared behind the manager, waving his receipt for the meal he had just paid for. The manager was immediately full of apologies at the mistake.

As they were going through the door, Colin turned and over the top of a couple going in, grabbed the manager by his suit lapels and tried to drag him outside. Johnny and Alan were quick to grab Colin and release the manager. Once outside, Colin was all for going back to the restaurant, but eventually common sense prevailed.

As they made their way back to Alan's car, Colin spotted a group of young men, one of them holding a greyhound on a tight lead. He went over and knelt in front of the dog and began to examine it closely. Johnny moved closer, just in case, and asked whose dog this was.

'I'm just looking after 'im,' the young man said grumpily.

Johnny grinned and said, 'Oh yeah? What does he do for 625 yards then?'

'I don't know, do I? He's not my bluddy dog!'

Colin got to his feet and said. 'He's not too bad for a greyhound, but give me a terrier every time.'

Turning away from the group, who had been silent throughout his examination, Colin gave the dog a friendly pat and followed Johnny and Alan back to where the car was parked.

Johnny opened the rear door and climbed in, at the same time motioning to Colin to get in the front seat. 'You'll get a better view of the road from there, Col.'

The drive back up the valley was quite smooth and almost silent as they climbed the long hill back to Rhyd-y-groes.

Alan brought the Jaguar to a gentle stop outside Colin's new abode.

He climbed out slowly, as if wanting to delay leaving the warmth and comfort of the leather seating. He leaned back into the car. 'Thank you, boys, for a great night out. I haven't enjoyed myself like that in a very long time. Thanks.'

CHAPTER 2

Johnny's grandfather

ON THE SATURDAY night following Colin's escapades in the Bird in Hand pub and later at the Chinese restaurant in Neath, the usual crowd of regulars in the bar were roaring with laughter when Johnny and Alan entered the room. Colin was on his feet with both hands outstretched as he described how he had been holding the manager's lapels while trying to pull him into the street over the heads of an unfortunate couple caught in the middle.

Trefor was the first to spot the pair and raised his voice to call them in, at the same time pointing to Colin, who had his back to them at that point in his story.

'You should 'ave seen, boys. The chap with the girl between us was doin' his best to duck under my bluddy arms but I was weighin' down on 'im and the manager was holdin' back with his hands on the door jamb. Then Alan...'

'...caught you by the scruff and pulled you back into the street!'

'Hey, boys!' Trefor shouted above the noise. 'Colin was just telling us about your escapades last night in Neath. I thought you two had more sense – and both of you councillors, too.'

Eyebrows raised, his round features broke into a broad smile. 'Two pints, is it?'

'Yes please, Tref, and a pint over for the cleckabox!' Alan grinned.

'Oh, 'ello Alan.' Colin grinned sheepishly and sat back down at the card table.

'C'mon, Col: finish the story then!' Bobby – his playing partner – said, grinning like the Cheshire Cat. 'He should finish the story, shouldn't he, boys?'

Amid calls from everyone around the table, Colin replied, 'Boys, there's no more to tell. We got back to Alan's car and we came home. Isn't that right, Alan?'

'Close enough.'

He turned around to face them, his narrow features creasing into a wide smile. 'Boys, it was a great night. The best I've 'ad for a long time, 'specially in the Bird in Hand. Hey, listen, I didn't tell you last night but I saw that bluddy woman again.' He paused, remembering. 'The one that me and Fred bought all those rum and blacks for, and when our backs were turned, she ran off with Dai Chops, the rotten sod.'

Seeing their puzzled expressions, he went on. 'Me and my father 'ad been buying her drinks all night in the hopes of one of us takin' her home, but she was too clever for that. She cwtched up to Dai and went off with 'im in his bluddy car and left us stranded for a while. Later when Dai came back for us, he told us that her 'usband was waitin' in the alley for her to come home and he was a yuge bloke, looked about 6' 6" or more and 20 stone, so Dai ran away. We 'ad a bluddy good laugh about that.'

Alan stared laughing. 'Aye, aye. I remember that one – he hasn't been in yere since, has he?'

'No, I don't think so. Anyway, she came up to me all dolled up, wearin' loads of make-up. So I asked her if she'd put it on with a trowel, is it?' He laughed in remembrance. 'She took a swing at me and missed, then she went into another room and I never saw her after.'

Johnny, who had moved to the far end of the bar where Trefor had placed his pint, took a sip and said, 'Trefor, believe this or not, but there was a pianist in the Bird in Hand who could be a double for Ben Turpin, the old film star. He had the most monumental squint and Colin wanted to know if he was looking at him and talking to me or looking at me and talking to him. I thought we were in trouble because the room went quiet. Me and Alan stood up with our backs to the wall expecting something to happen but luckily for us this chap had a sense of humour and started laughing and began playing the piano again. Talk about old Fred causing a row wherever he went! Colin is no slouch either! I think he could cause a row in an empty room!'

Trefor and the crowd standing at the bar roared with laughter at that one.

'Hey, Colin,' Elwyn shouted across the room. 'I see you've got your name in this week's *Aberdare Leader* again.'

'Oh, aye? What was it this time? Something about me shootin' a fox over by Cwmdare a few weeks back? Me and Jimmy were comin' home across the top *waun* from Cwmdare after we'd shot a couple of rabbits, when this bluddy fox rose from right under our feet. I was a bit in front of Jimmy in the long grass and took a shot at it from 30 or 40 yards. We found it was a vixen I 'ad shot and we could tell she 'ad cubs, so we spent a bit of time looking for them but never found anything. Jimmy thought she 'ad been travellin' from somewhere else, so I cut off her tail for the Farmers' Fox Destruction Club. It was dark by the time we got home too.'

Trefor, who had been listening to the story, called out. 'Hey boys! I don't think it was about foxes. I believe I read that it was about that big marker stone you boys found between the Mardy Water and Padell y Bwlch a while ago.'

'Oh, that one! That was ages ago.' Colin chipped in. 'There was a crowd of us that day, Tref. Aye, aye. I remember it now. A mate of George Teale, a lawyer, looked it up. It was from the time of the Enclosure Act, when people with money fenced off common land and resold it. At least, that is how I think it worked.'

'Yes,' Trefor added. 'You can bet a lot of money was made off that land, whoever owned it.'

'You're right enough, Trefor,' Johnny said, turning towards the bar. 'I remember reading about it in school, years and years ago. That *waun* from Waun-gron down as far as Cwmdare was once – many years ago, mind – common grazing land for anyone living in the area who owned any cattle or sheep. My grandfather had one of the clerks from his engineering shop write out by hand who all the parcels of land were sold to from Waun-gron all the way to Cwmdare. I've seen the ledger, it's still in the family somewhere. Yes, Trefor. My grandfather had a big haulage company, too, and employed a lot of local people.'

'How many did he employ, Johnny?'

'Oh, I don't know that. I do know that he did a lot of clever things about the place. He hauled all sorts of things from the Pandy all the way down to Abercynon basin to load on the barges down there, which eventually made their way down to the docks in Cardiff.'

'Oh, I remember now,' Trefor murmured. 'You're a Rowe! You're from one of the oldest families in Waun-gron.'

'Yes,' Johnny smiled. 'And through my grandmother I am distantly belonging to the Watkins Fforch y Garon and the Walters Bryn Siriol and somehow to the old people who once lived at Pant Hendre Bach.'

Trefor reached his outstretched hand over the bar and he and Johnny solemnly shook hands.

'Yes Tref, my grandfather was clever all right. One day a chap living in Waun-gron came to his home almost in tears. The bungalow he and his wife and family lived in had somehow been built on next door's land. Apparently, he and his family had lived in this house for more than 30 years or more, and only when the place next door had been sold and the new owner asked a surveyor to set out his property boundary lines was the mistake discovered. He told my grandfather that now the new owner wanted to knock his bungalow down to make way for something else.

'My *tad-cu* asked this chap how much over the boundary it was. I think he said it was only about three feet. Well, my *tad-cu* calmed him down a bit and told him that he would come up to his place to have a look at his problem. In the end he told the old chap that he could move his bungalow onto a new site on his own land and not to worry about a thing. Of course, the old chap was overjoyed at the news! But he then asked my *tad-cu* if he would have to empty everything out of his home for the proposed move. *Tad-cu* told him to leave everything just as it is.'

Trefor raised his eyebrows, at the same time asking, 'How in the world did he do that?'

'Well, it sounds easy today but remember this was in the late twenties. He jacked up the whole bungalow and fitted some rails underneath and slid the whole house onto the new site they had already prepared without disturbing a single thing inside. Yes, he was a very clever chap all right.

'I'll tell you another thing he did.' Johnny was now warming to the subject of his grandfather. 'He went up to a place somewhere up in north Wales to look at a moving job some of the biggest haulage companies in the country had said was impossible. It involved moving a yuge piece of equipment across the main railway line without shutting down the rail service in that particular area. Well, he was there for a couple of days studying the site and the timetable he had to work with. He did his calculations and said it could be done as requested.

'Later, when the job was finished to everyone's satisfaction, he was given a presentation by the company who hired him, for his ability and efficiency in doing the job within the time allowed.' He smiled at the landlord's expression of incredulity.

They both turned in the direction of the card table where a sudden noise was coming from. Colin was on his feet again, describing once more how he had gripped the unfortunate manager of the Chinese restaurant.

Trefor reached out for Old John Shinkins' glass, as he came towards the bar shaking his head and pointing in Colin's direction. 'He'll never change, Tref. Never – *byth*.'

CHAPTER 3

Croesfordd Community Centre

I<small>T WAS</small> T<small>UESDAY</small> evening and the monthly Parish Council meeting was about to begin promptly at seven o'clock. The room in Croesfordd Community Centre had been prepared in advance with a long table for the committee at one end of the room, flanked on both sides by comfortable easy chairs.

On the long table facing the other members sat Bill Thomas, the Clerk; to his left, Johnny Wills, the Chairman; and further to his left, Alan George, the Vice-Chairman.

Johnny rapped sharply on the table with his knuckles to bring the meeting to order and in the first order of business asked the Clerk to read the minutes of the last meeting. These were dutifully read and the meeting was asked if there was anything arising from the minutes. There being nothing, they moved through the agenda and finally came to Any Other Business.

'Is there any correspondence we need to discuss tonight?' Johnny asked.

Bill Thomas, the Clerk, said, 'Yes, Mr Chairman. We have received a letter from Neath Rural District Council.' He hesitated momentarily, before reading out loud, '*To: Rhyd-y-groes Parish*

Council: We understand that your Council is in possession of a 20-acre parcel of land that is at present not being used…

'Mr Chairman, ladies and gentlemen, let me explain. This 20-acre parcel is land that was ceded to us for our parishioners to use as common land, such as allotments or the grazing of any stock they might have. There is a local farmer who annually cuts the grass for the hay and pays a nominal sum to us for the crop. To my knowledge we have never made use of it in this capacity and neither have any of our parishioners, at least not since I have been Clerk of this Council. I have taken the trouble to look through old records and minutes going back before the last war and found nothing. Of course, there could be reference to this land in those records in the County Archives in Cardiff but…' He shrugged his shoulders.

Johnny looked at the Clerk and sensed there was something else. 'Perhaps we could have a look at the letter and its contents before we dig too deep into this request, Bill. Please continue.'

'Oh, most certainly, Mr Chairman. It reads:

To: Rhyd-y-groes Parish Council.

We understand that your Council is in possession of a 20-acre parcel of land that is at present not being used…

'Yere they provide the exact ordnance survey location, adjoining the A465 west of Waun-gron.

We, the Neath Rural District Council Planning office, would like to know if the Rhyd-y-groes Parish Council have any objection to us giving outline planning permission to install an Industrial facility, namely a Gas Pumping Station, on this land?'

Johnny looked quickly at Alan, then at the other members. 'Mmm. Something is not quite right yere, Bill! Do you have any clue what's behind this letter? No? Well, it seems pretty vague to me. I'll put this to the council right now for open discussion.'

Frank Knott stood up. 'Well, Mr Chairman, correct me if I'm wrong, but we have had some dealings in the past with the

Neath Planning lot and some of their decisions have not been to our liking at all. I think we should investigate this request thoroughly before we agree to anything.'

'Well said, Frank,' said Johnny. 'Let us say this: We agree in principle to have outline planning given to our land. It may come in handy for some future project that could be of some benefit to our community, but – and it is a large BUT – we want to know a lot more about this project before we commit to anything. Are we all in agreement so far? Can I have a show of hands, please? Bill, please make a note that the whole Parish Council is in agreement that Neath Rural District Planning Department are to provide us with a fully detailed explanation of this gas pumping station. In the meantime, as the District Councillor for this area, I will try and find out as much as I can about this so-called "facility" the next time I am in Neath.'

'Duly noted, Mr Chairman.' The Clerk quickly wrote in his notes as requested.

'Do we have any other business?'

'None at this time, Mr Chairman.'

'In that case, I declare this meeting closed.' Johnny rapped once on the table.

He stretched upwards, easing the ache in his back. 'I'm a member of the District Council as you know but... well, you know what I mean, Al.'

'Yep! We'll just have to wait and see what they're up to. Whatever it is, they can't hide it forever.'

Outside, as they walked towards Alan's car, Johnny said, 'I think Bill has yerd something on the grapevine – you know how it is, office gossip – but he can't say anything just in case it's wrong and he loses his job. He's worked hard to get where he is as Head of Department and, of course, I'm pretty sure he will be retiring in a few years. To be fair, he can't put all that in jeopardy. Besides, I'm only *thinking* that he might know something but can't openly say anything about it – but I've been wrong before.'

Alan smiled and patted him on his broad shoulder. 'Yes, you have, Johnny, but it's not for me to remind you, is it?'

At that moment, Bill Thomas came out of the Community Centre, hugging his heavy, overstuffed briefcase to his chest. Johnny called out, 'Can we give you a lift, Bill?'

A relieved smile lit up his features. 'Gentlemen, I would appreciate that no end. Thank you. I'm most obliged.'

Alan started his powerful Jaguar and slipped it into gear. 'We're thinking of going to the Plough for one pint, Bill. Just the one. Do you want to join us for a glass of light ale?'

'Thank you, Alan, but no thank you. It's been a very long day and the comfort of my bed is calling me.'

In silence they drove the nearly two miles to Bill Thomas' house, wished him a good night's rest and turned the car in the direction of the Plough Inn.

Entering the smoke-filled main bar, the first person they saw, sitting resplendent in a light-blue pinstripe suit, which clearly stood out against the drab working clothes of the other men, was Bandit!

'David Samuel Noel Goliath Jones! Where in the world have you sprung from? I haven't seen you in yere f'rages!' Alan smiled broadly as he posed the question.

Bandit opened his mouth to reply but Johnny got in there first. 'He's been to see his tailor at Swansea nick, Alan, as evidenced by his new clobber,' Johnny laughed. 'What happened this time?'

'Well, I 'ad to go to court again and William Rees, who was the judge that day, asked me why I was always in debt. So, I told 'im. I wasn't getting enough money and the little pullet – my wife – likes to spend a bit. Then he said, "You must make greater efforts to curb your spending, Mr Jones." So, then I told 'im we 'ad a system in our house: we put all the names who we owed money to in a hat and if any one of them nagged us to get paid, we didn't put their names in the hat for the next month. The people in the court started laughing, which I think annoyed 'im a bit. He looked at me and said, nasty like, "28 days inside!" And that's what 'appened this time, Johnny.'

There wasn't an ounce of harm in the man, even though he was in and out of jail on a fairly regular basis – mainly because he couldn't keep out of debt, and the local Magistrates' Court frowned on that.

'I'll put a pint over the bar for you, David – good to see you home,' said Johnny, smiling.

Bandit gave a toothless smile and inclined his head in deference to Johnny's generosity.

'So, what happened to your new teeth, then?' Johnny asked.

'Our bluddy dog ate them.'

The crowd around the table erupted in laughter.

'What! Your dog ate them? I don't believe that, not for one minute,' Johnny said laughing. 'It's a good story, though.'

'Boys, it's right enough what I'm tellin' you, as God is my judge. Cos they were new, I took them out to 'ave a spell and put them on the arm of the chair. Next thing that bluddy dog of ours grabbed them and ran to hide in the back of our big sofa. You've seen that one, Alan. It's too 'eavy for one man to shift and by the time I got one of my boys to 'elp to move it, my bluddy teeth 'ad gone. That's God's truth, boys!'

'Come off it, Bandit! The Health Service people will never believe that story,' Johnny laughed. 'Did you hear that, Tref?'

'I did, and I've yerd some good ones in yere in my time, especially from the likes of old Fred and a few others, but that has to be one of the best yet.'

'And I'll tell you another thing,' Bandit cut in, 'believe it or not, when our dog 'ad her pups not long after, every one of those pups 'ad teeth!'

The crowd in the bar totally erupted, howling with laughter.

'It's right enough, what I'm saying,' Bandit stood up and raised his voice above the noise.

Johnny went over to the bar, shaking his head. 'Trefor, this place is priceless! Have you ever yerd such a thing? Give me that pint, please, and I'll take it over to him.'

Pint in hand, he returned to the card table. 'Yere you are, Mr Jones, with my compliments. So, what else have you been up to since you have returned to the fold, so to speak?'

'Ah. Let's see. When I came home the little pullet started complaining that her stove wouldn't work anymore and that she'd been doing cooking on the fireplace. I said there was nothing wrong with that, which led to a big row about me enjoying myself in the nick while she struggled to keep our home and family together. Anyway, I had a few pounds in my pocket and went down to Aberdare and I saw this stove in a shop window on sale with twelve easy payments. So, I went in and signed up for it. They didn't even ask for a deposit and they must have been in a hurry to get rid of it because they delivered it the next day with a fitter to put it in. Well, he took the old one out and then struggled by 'imself to get the new one in. Then he asked me where the tap was, so I got 'im a glass of water. He said, "I don't want any bluddy water, I want to know where your damn gas connection is!" I told him we don't 'ave any gas in Rhyd-y-groes. That's when he got mad and asked me why I 'ad signed up for a gas stove! I didn't know it was a bluddy gas stove. I don't know anything about bluddy stoves, do I? I bet he was as mad as 'ell taking that stove out of our house and back to the shop in Aberdare.'

Again, the crowd erupted in hysterical laughter at his innocent-sounding revelations.

Alan, holding his sides as if in pain, said, 'Bandit, you're the bluddy limit and that story is worth a free pint. Trefor, put a pint over for this gentleman, please, and I'll pay for it when I come up to the bar.'

As one, Alan and Johnny made their way to their usual spot at the far end of the bar, where they could talk in relative peace and quiet with the landlord.

'Trefor, this place is like a comedy show! They all say that laughter is the best medicine, don't they? Look at Old John Shinkins over there holding his sides and coughing his heart out. I'll bet he hasn't laughed like that in years. Well, maybe not years, but at least since old Fred passed away. He too was hell of a boy, mind. As I said about him to Colin the other day, Fred could cause a row in an empty room, just as easy as that.' He snapped his fingers.

'So, boys, what's new in the council meeting tonight then?'

Johnny and Alan looked at each other and Alan shrugged. Johnny said, 'Well, we've had an inquiry from Neath Rural and they want to give outline planning on that piece of land the Parish Council owns down by the NCB washery. It's about 20 acres and we're always wary when they put forward something like this with no real details – more than a bit suspicious of their motives. We'll get to the bottom of it in the end, you mark my words.' He lifted his glass to finish the last half pint and said. 'I don't know about you, Alan, but I'm ready to go home.'

'C'mon Johnny, let's have another one before we go. Remember what Fred used to say: "A bird can't fly on one wing." Two pints of bitter, Tref.'

Johnny smiled wryly. 'Aye, you're right enough. Why would we want to leave yere with all this fun going on? I'm just glad Trefor yere doesn't charge an entrance fee for all this entertainment.'

Trefor looked up from pulling the pints. 'Now, that's a really good idea, Johnny! I might look into that.' His round features were wreathed in a broad smile as he placed the foaming glasses in front of them.

Some time later, Johnny looked at the large clock that hung on the wall behind the bar. 'I don't know about you, Al, but I am just about ready to go home. See, it's almost closing time.' He raised his glass and swallowed the remains of his last pint with a sigh of satisfaction. 'And we were only going to have the one, weren't we?'

'Yes, we were, but it's all good fun in yere. It's almost a shame to leave, innit?' Alan smiled, placing his empty glass on the bar. 'I suppose we'll see you later in the week, Tref. Goodnight, all.'

CHAPTER 4

Remembering Fred

'FIFTEEN TWO, FIFTEEN four and two is six and six is a dozen.' In quiet tones the score was being announced when Alan got up from his seat at the end of the large farmhouse table in the Plough and rapped sharply on the homemade scoreboard. This signified that he and his partner Johnny would be challenging the winners for a pint a corner on the next game. Empty glass in hand, he was making his way towards the bar when he stopped suddenly and turned back towards the card table, and said in a loud voice:

'Hey, boys! Do you know what tomorrow is?'

'Aye, Alan,' Bobby said with a laugh. 'It's Wednesday, mun.'

'I'm not talking about that, you *twpsyn*! Tomorrow is two years to the day that we buried Fred! Isn't that right, Colin?'

Colin, his cap pulled down tightly to his ears and shading his eyes, looked up from the card game. 'You're right enough, Alan. It is exactly two years to the very day. Damn, I still miss the old so and so, mind. Between us, we 'ad such a lot of fun…'

'And beer!' Trefor called out across the room, from behind the bar.

'That too,' Colin replied agreeably. 'That too! Boys, he was a lot of fun to be around, especially when he was on form.'

'I remember one time when he brought a chicken home from somewhere down in Waun-gron. He said he'd bought it pretty cheap but I thought at the time that p'raps he'd found it lyin' around after it 'ad died from old age, cos it was as tough as 'ell to chew. What I'm tellin' you is right enough! Boys, even the bluddy gravy was tough!'

The crowd around the table broke into fits of laughter as Colin, with a wry smile on his thin features, scooped up the cards to deal out another hand. 'No, boys, I'm only saying. He was 'ell of a boy and we did 'ave a lot of fun wherever we ended up. He knew such a lot of people – or at least they knew 'im, especially after he got banned from yere by Trefor.' He looked across the room at the landlord and raised his cap in mock salute to him. 'Remember that time, Tref?'

Trefor, drying glasses at the far end of the bar, just grinned and said, 'Yes, I do, Colin, and I have to say that I was a bit sorry after, but he'd made me so angry with what he did! Der, *bois bach!*' Trefor said, raising his eyebrows. 'Fred could cause a row with anyone without even trying...'

'Ugh, don't – *paid sôn!*' Colin interrupted, putting his cards face down on the table. 'Just listen to this! It was in those first two weeks after the ban that we started to go to the New Inn for a few pints. Well, it was quite a bit closer to our cottage at the Mount than it would 'ave been walkin' to the Plough, but we couldn't 'ave any strap there so we didn't drink as much. Which might 'ave been a good thing for both of us.

'But my father made up for that pretty quick cos the New Inn was right on the A465 main road and 'ad a lot of passing trade. Fred, the cheeky sod, would go up to complete strangers, if he 'ad a chance, and say, 'You don't know who I am, do you?' Then he would start into some story about his younger days huntin' foxes, and some of his exploits as a young man on the farms down in Waun-gron. His favourite tale, was of course, about the "Funny Money" and how he decided to call 'imself the "Dollar Boy" – 'member that one? Der, he got loads of free beer out of that one! He would tell that one over and over 'til they got fed up with 'im and bought 'im a pint, just to get rid of 'im.

'Hey, Alan! You must remember this! It was one Sunday morning back then, when you and Johnny came down into the darts room at the New Inn. It was when me and Fred was tellin' the boys about my father's old nonsense from the night before at the sheep sales at the Red Lion in Penderyn. Der, there was a place! He almost caused a riot in there with his nonsense. He was spouting about his inside knowledge on farming and offering advice to everyone around 'im and almost got us thrown out of the bluddy pub. He 'ad told one farmer that he knew that one of the local boys 'ad managed to sell his almost blind horse to someone at the last sale – not realising that the farmer he was talking to was the one who 'ad bought it! This farmer was ready to punch Fred's lights out for making him look a bluddy fool in front of all his friends there.

'Then, not learning anything from that fright, Fred went on to point out to another farmer how he 'ad been caught out by another local farmer, buying his poor-quality bull!'

Colin and everyone listening in was laughing. 'Oh, the tales about my father and his silly nonsense are endless. I hear some of them nearly every day in work and in the pubs in Waun-gron, Penderyn and even down in Glynneath.'

'Yes, I remember that Sunday morning, Col. C'mon Alan! You must remember that time! We'd just come into the long room when Danny Davies came in to throw some practice darts.'

'Aye, aye. I remember it now. You're right enough. That must be three years ago now!'

'Aye, aye! That's the day. Anyway, the row in the Red Lion didn't amount to much in the end cos my father started singin' "There's a Bridle Hanging on the Wall" right in the middle of everyone shoutin' their 'eads off in the bar, and before you knew it, he 'ad everyone singin' with him. Then, on top of all the nonsense he 'ad caused, the landlady gave 'im a pint for calmin' things down. I told Fred at the time, he should 'ave 'ad a clout on the side of his head for 'avin' cheek enough to take the pint off her, considerin' he was the one who 'ad started it all in the first place!'

'P'raps she should have given you a bang on the side of your head too, for taking him there in your car in the first place.'

'C'mon, Johnny, fair play! My father could cause a row with the Pope without even tryin', everybody knows that!' At that, everyone broke up in stitches, laughing and enjoying the moment.

'And talking of clergymen, listen to this one. Me and Fred were in the Red Lion one day in the summer, sittin' by the front window, when this clergyman from Waun-gron looked in and saw Fred. So he came into the bar and stood by our table lookin' down on us. Fred pretended he wasn't there and took a good swig of his beer. This vicar, or whoever he was, started speakin' in a stern voice to my father. He said he knew all about my mother leavin' us to go and live back in Waun-gron, and so on. Then he started to speak to my father about families and how they should be livin' together and all that.

'Fred, lookin' at me, pulled a face behind his hand while pretendin' to listen to him. Then he said to the vicar: "I'd like to buy you a pint of best bitter so that you can sit down with us yere and 'ave a good old chat."

'I looked at Fred all gone out, and wondered what he was playin' at now. Anyway, this vicar bloke thanked Fred and said he didn't drink beer. So, Fred said, "That's okay, I'll get you a light shandy. It's mostly pop anyway," he told him. Fred went up to the bar and came back with a pint for the vicar, which he drank pretty quickly. Fred then went to get 'im another shandy.

'Well boys, in no time at all, the vicar was all over the place. His words were comin' out all jumbled, he was slurrin' others, his fancy church hat was on sideways and he couldn't sit straight on his chair. Finally, he got up in a bit of a rush and left us in peace. I 'spect he had a really bad 'ead the followin' day. Good thing, though, that it was a weekday and not a Saturday. I 'ave never in my life seen anythin' like it after just two pints of shandy!

'So, I asked my father what 'ad 'appened. He said he'd bought a pint of best bitter and 'ad taken a good swig out of it, then added a small bottle of IPA to each pint! Well, we all know how strong that is, especially for someone who doesn't drink beer. We 'ad a good laugh about that.

'Fred said after, "I don't think he'll want to 'ave a chat with me again!"'

Johnny said, 'I remember that! I said to Fred at the time, "You bought a devout churchman beer?" And he replied, "Why not, indeed? He puts his trousers on the same way as me, don't he?"'

All those listening to the tale began laughing as their imagination ran away with them, picturing the poor clergyman trying to explain what had happened to him after meeting Fred in the Red Lion pub.

At that point, Johnny took up the story with another caper from that same day. 'Boys, I remember as if it was yesterday. Danny came into the long room and went straight to the dartboard, where he began putting paper flights in his darts. Der, there's a darter for you! He was among the best around yere. Yes, he should have been entered into the News of the World Darts Tournament, he was that good. Alan and me and a few of the boys went up to Ally Pally one time to see Bill Harding from Waun-gron play in it. I think he got to the semi-finals too. Anyway, when Mrs Lewis, the landlady, came down from the bar in the tap room, he asked for a pint and then asked if anybody in the room would like to have a game. As I recall, there were no takers. "It's only for a bit of fun, boys,' Danny said, 'just to make a bit of practice interesting, that's all."'

Colin began laughing. 'Aye, aye, that's right! Fred said, "Not me!" I don't think he could throw snowballs tidy but he was brilliant with a shotgun in his 'ands.' He rolled back in his chair, laughing until the tears ran down his face at some hidden meaning in his words.

Johnny again took up the tale. 'So, Danny turned away from the group at the table and began throwing dart after dart at the treble-twenty slot, hitting the narrow area time after time. He was deadly, boys! Then for some reason,known only to him, Fred got up from his chair and went over to stand right behind Danny as he continued throwing dart after dart at the same spot.

'"Got a game tonight, 'ave you?" Fred asked him.

'"Aye. Over in the Rhondda," Danny replied, not taking his eyes off the board. The darts kept thudding into the treble-twenty. And this is where Fred tried to wind him up. He said, "Hey, Danny! That's bluddy good throwing, mun!" He turned and winked at us watching his antics, and we knew him well enough to know he was up to something again.

'"Pity you don't look as good as those darts you're throwing."

'"What the 'ell are you bothering about now then, Fred?" Danny turned to look directly at him, as if trying to make some sense from his words.

'"I said, pity..."

'Then Danny said he knew very well what Fred had said and he wanted to know what he had meant by it, that's all. Of course, Fred couldn't answer that without giving the game away: he had a measuring tape cwtched in his hand, so he said nothing but continued to watch as dart after dart flew into the treble-twenty slot.

'At the time, Alan, me and Bandit could see the funny side of your father's antics with his tape measure,' said Johnny, 'but I think that Danny might have caught a glimpse of Fred trying to take a measurement behind his back. In the end though, he suddenly stopped throwing, put his darts away and with a nod to us, he left the room like he had wings on his feet.

'Fred had to have the last word on Danny's hurried departure. He said, "There's a spoilsport for you. We could 'ave 'ad a bit more fun with 'im if he 'adn't caught on that I was winding 'im up."

'It was then he went to sit down on the bench by Alan. He pulled out a packet of five Wills Woodbines and said, "Sorry, boys, last one," and, a minute later when he thought no one was watching him, he picked up the empty packet and put it back in the side pocket of his jacket. Colin, I'd seen your father doing this before when we went rabbiting over in Llyswen, the other side of Talgarth – you were there with me, Jimmy, and Titch. I only have to say to Titch, "Remember the Brecon Hotel?" and he breaks up, saying he remembers that day just like yesterday. What a laugh that was.

'Anyway, to get back to the story of that Sunday – Alan thought this was a bit of a funny thing to do. Right Al?

'Aye, it was,' Alan grinned, taking up the story. 'So when Fred picked up his pint to take a swig about five minutes later, I looked down and his side pocket was gaping open right there, so I dipped my fingertips into it and came out with a packet of five Wills Woodbines, then I did it again and brought out another packet of five Woodbines. I did this a number of times without Fred even noticing, until I had about ten packets on the bench beside me. I raised my hand to get Johnny's attention and pointed to all these packets on the bench. I turned my head slightly away from Fred and opened each of the packets and found just one cigarette in each of them. So, I began to lay them out in front of me in a straight line across the table – right in front of your father, Col – and said to everyone around the table, "Well, what do you think, boys? Now we all know how he does it." At the same time, I pointed to the display of the pale green five-Woodbine packets spread across the table.'

'Right enough, Al. That was when I chipped in and said loud enough for him to hear, "Hey, Fred! How about you passing around the cigarettes! It must be your turn by now!"

'And then you said, "No, no! Don't bother him about giving out his cigarettes now, Johnny. You know Fred is always short of ciggies! Yere, have one of these Wills Woodbines instead. They are free today!"

'At that, Fred seemed to suddenly wake up and jumped to his feet, banging his half-full pint glass on the table, splashing beer all over the place. "Hey! Wait a bluddy minute yere! They look like my bluddy cigarettes!" he said, patting the outside of his side pockets.

'"So how do you know that for sure then, Fred?" Alan asked, smiling up at him. "Do you have your name on them anywhere, or on every cigarette?"

'"No, I don't!" Fred blustered, his cheeks turning a nice shade of red, "but that's always the way I keep my cigarettes. I think it helps to keep the tobacco dry."

'What a brilliant excuse, boys! Have you ever heard anything like that before?'

'Oh, aye,' said Colin, with a grin. 'My father 'ad an answer for everythin', and he was pretty quick with it too.'

'As I remember it, Alan, you laughed at him and he got pretty embarrassed, if that is the right word to use for Fred, when you said, "That must be why you always say, 'Sorry, boys, my last one!' You must spend half your time collecting empty 5-Woodbine packets, Fred."

'"No, no! It's not like that!" Fred was trying his hardest to regain his composure in light of everybody knowing what he was up to. "It's just handier to carry them like that and then I don't smoke as many in a day." Then he scooped up all the packets in one movement and dropped them back in his pocket with a flourish.

'Yes, boys,' added Johnny, a distant look in his eyes as he remembered once again that hilarious Sunday morning. 'We always had a bit of fun with Fred around. You could never tell what he was going to do or say next.'

'Aye, he had 'ell of a sense of humour too!' Alan joined in. 'He said he got it from his mother. After talking about him with his daughter Sheila, I asked him one time where he had been born. He said he was born in St Davids down in Pembrokeshire, on St David's Day, and his mother decided to call him FRED! I thought about it after and couldn't think of any other name for him. Can you imagine him being called Clarence or Ebenezer or Gerald?'

The crowd around the cribbage table broke into fits of laughter at that.

Colin picked up his cards. 'Yes, you're right enough, Johnny. Whose turn was it, boys? I forgot where we were, with all this talk about my father.'

'It's my lead,' said Bobby. 'We need just four holes to peg out, and it will be my first take and I'm holding a dozen.'

CHAPTER 5

The Butcher and the 38 lb Turkey

As THE LAST few days of March approached, Trefor Plough, ever the practical joker, turned his thoughts towards Rhys Rees the butcher and how to pay him back for all the aggravation he'd caused him over the last twelve months – and by phoning Trefor once again at 3.00 a.m. that morning. He made himself a cup of tea and sat in his easy chair in front of the Aga stove, turning over in his mind one scheme after another. 'All I have to do is wait,' he decided, 'and he'll provide me with the opportunity. I just cannot understand the man or why he's doing this: it's absolute nonsense to either sit up till all hours to call me or get out of bed for the same purpose, just to annoy me. Why?'

Later in the day, he heard on the grapevine that his former butcher had recently quarrelled with the landlord of a large hotel situated in the valley below Rhyd-y-groes. If the story was true, the butcher had been told in no uncertain manner, 'Get out, and don't come back in yere until I tell you to!' It only needed this little gem of information to send Trefor's creative mind into high gear.

Immediately he began putting all the bits and pieces of information together and thought, 'With any luck, I can get him *and* his stepbrother with this one.'

Late on the Tuesday afternoon, he called the butcher's stepbrother WIll David's office, knowing full well that he would have already left for the day, and asked his secretary if she would be good enough to speak to Will first thing in the morning and give him the following message:

'This is Mr Ben Williams, Manager of the Rose and Crown up in the Neath valley. I've been trying to contact Rhys Rees, your boss' stepbrother: he's our local butcher, you know, but for some reason I cannot locate him. So, I thought, since I know your boss, Will David, quite well, perhaps he could let Mr Rhys Rees, the butcher, know this as soon as possible.

'Thing is, I have some guests staying in my hotel who are from Texas, and to tell you the truth, I'm a bit fed up with their constant bragging about how every single thing is so much bigger and better over there in the United States. Well, they have made a request for a turkey dinner for this coming Friday, and I was wondering if Mr Rees could provide me with the biggest turkey he can find. I don't care how big it is: the bigger, the better would suit me. Perhaps something in the range of 30 lb, or bigger if he can find one. This is important. I need to know as soon as possible if he can help me, otherwise I will have to look elsewhere.

'If you could be good enough to tell your boss first thing in the morning, I would be most obliged, and if Mr Rees does have a suitable turkey, ask if he could bring it over tomorrow morning?

'Now, I want to make sure you have all the details, because we don't want these Yanks to think we can't put on a bit of a show yere in Wales, do we? So, please read back all that I have said in my message.'

She did exactly as he had requested. He thanked her profusely for her accuracy and carefully replaced the handset. Now all he had to do was wait for his scheme to materialise.

He knew that every Tuesday the butcher's stepbrother Will was out all day, delivering orders for Rhys Rees to some of the farms and outlying areas of the parish and would, most likely, be out of contact with everyone.

And so, early on that Tuesday morning, just as he was about to leave on his rounds, he received the urgent message from his secretary, as dictated to her by Trefor Plough. He immediately called his stepbrother's home and relayed the message he had received word for word, and then asked, 'But I don't know – where the 'ell would you be able to get a bird that big on such short notice?'

The butcher laughed out loud. 'What a bluddy stroke of luck!' he shouted down the phone. 'Would you believe it? I've got one such bird in the freezer at the back of my shop. I got it as a special order a couple of months ago for a Christmas party, but they let me down at the last minute and I haven't had a chance to get rid of it since then. If I remember, this one is about 38 lbs, so it will be just right for those Yanks.' He began laughing again. 'Best of all, I'll be able to charge Ben Williams top price, too! Thanks for the tip-off, *brawd*!' He replaced the handset and sat for a few minutes working out, in his mind, what he needed to do first. Then, putting his thoughts into action, he went quickly to his shop and retrieved the turkey from the freezer and placed it on the counter, in readiness to deliver it later that morning. He stood back to admire the enormous bird and rubbed his hands in anticipation of a tidy profit.

At exactly 11.15 a.m. he carried the partly thawed turkey out to his delivery van and made his way quickly down the valley road to the Rose and Crown Hotel. He entered the bar by the front door just moments after the manager, Ben Williams, had opened for business. He staggered slightly as he embraced the huge bird, holding it firmly to his chest with both hands , then dropped it with a loud bang on the polished mahogany bar.

Turning quickly towards the sudden noise, Ben Williams looked with a puzzled expression from the huge bird to the butcher and then back again. His eyes widened in amazement at the sight of the partially frozen turkey on the bar.

'What the...?' he started to say, when he suddenly remembered his last encounter with Rhys Rees. 'HEY! What are YOU doing in yere? Didn't I tell you the last time I spoke to you, not to come back in yere until I told you so? Do you remember that?'

'Well, yes, but I thought it was okay now because I got your urgent message this morning and I've brought you this big turkey you asked for!'

'Turkey? What the 'ell are you blathering about, mun? What urgent message? I haven't left any message for you about anything and certainly not any message about a bluddy turkey, that's for sure!'

The butcher stood and stared at him with a blank expression on his florid face and started to get that sinking feeling that something was very wrong here. 'But... but you left a message with my stepbrother,' he insisted, grabbing at any straw in the whirlwind that was about to engulf him. 'You said you wanted to show these Yanks from Texas a yuge turkey for their dinner, didn't you?'

'What Yanks? There are no bluddy Yanks in yere, nor have I seen any. You are the biggest bluddy turkey around yere. Now get out and stay out! The both of you,' he added, pointing to the huge turkey, dripping moisture onto the bar in the warmth of the room. 'Hey! I've told you to go, now go on! Get out of yere when I'm telling you!'

The butcher stood stock still with the colour draining from his florid cheeks as it slowly dawned on him what day it was. 'It's April the First,' he whispered, as if to himself; then louder. 'It's April the bluddy First!'

'What's that? What did you just say?'

'I said its April the First,' he repeated. 'That bluddy Trefor Plough! I'm going to bluddy kill him!' he shouted, grabbing the turkey off the bar with both hands. He spun on his heels and charged back out through the open door.

Ben Williams just stood there, laughing until the tears ran down his cheeks. He called his wife Annie to relate the story of the butcher and the huge turkey.

By open tap that evening, the story had got back to the Plough Inn. Rhys Rees, of course, was absolutely livid at being bested once again by Trefor Plough. He couldn't prove it was Trefor, but in his mind, he just knew. He called his stepbrother Will to try and get to the bottom of the elaborate prank, but he was away somewhere playing rugby. By now, the butcher was absolutely tampin' at not being able to call anyone to complain. On the spur of the moment, he decided to call Trefor at the Plough Inn.

'Hello? Waun-gron 252,' Trefor said quietly into the phone.

'I'll get you for this, you bluddy swine!' came the shouted response.

Trefor knew in an instant who was on the other end of the line, but he politely replied, 'I'm sorry, but I'm not sure I quite follow you, sir.' He held the phone away from his ear.

'I'm going to get you, Trefor Plough!' the butcher screamed down the phone. 'Making a fool of me again, is it?'

'And who is this, please?' Trefor asked in his politest tone, then held the phone away from him at the crude reply.

'You know very well who this is, Trefor Plough, but I'm going to get you for this! You mark my words!' Rhys Rees said threateningly, slamming down the phone in temper.

'*Duw, Duw*!' Trefor murmured to himself. 'Well! There's upset he is.'

In the bar later that night, the main story on everyone's lips was about Rhys Rees the butcher and the oversize turkey. Of course, there were numerous distortions of the truth and some outlandish additions to the actual event. Everybody was looking to the landlord to confirm or deny every bit of information as it arrived in the bar of the Plough. Trefor, for his part, politely refused to be drawn into any discussion and when really pressed for an answer, all he would say was, 'Well, fancy that. I wonder who would do such a thing to him, of all people?'

After a while, the subject of the butcher and his turkey came to an end and the general conversation turned to other topics, such as who were the best darts players in the parish or who had picked the most winners from the horse racing the previous Saturday, and then, who had the best tips for the following day's racing at Chepstow.

Colin looked up from the card table and said in a loud voice, 'All this bluddy noise about horses and winners. If my father was still alive today, he would mark everyone's card for the runners at Chepstow!'

It was like the straw that broke the camel's back. The bar erupted into one huge clamour as everyone aired their opinions on horse racing and Fred's dubious advice.

Trefor beamed, nodding to Colin and indicating there was a pint over the bar for him. This was just the sort of atmosphere he enjoyed.

CHAPTER 6

Trefor's Little Green Van

THE NEXT DAY, a Wednesday early in December, there was a home game at the Gnoll in Neath with a 2.30 p.m. kick-off. Afterwards, Johnny volunteered to drive Alan's Jaguar back up the valley. He found it quite exhilarating guiding the powerful machine through the darkening winding valley roads and up the long hill to Rhyd-y-groes. At the top of the hill, there being no other traffic in sight, he swung the big car across the road and into the narrower village road and down the hill towards the Plough Inn. As he carefully negotiated one of the blind corners, Alan spotted in the glow of their headlights a small green Morris van tilted sideways in the shallow ditch.

'Hey! Wait a minute, Johnny! I think that was Trefor's little van in the ditch back there!'

Johnny immediately took his foot off the accelerator with the intention of turning around to see if it was indeed Trefor's van.

'No, no!' Alan said quickly. 'You'll have 'ell of a job trying to turn this car round in this narrow road. Keep going: we'll see soon enough when we get to the Plough.' Minutes later, Johnny turned the Jag into the car park alongside the Plough. There was no sign of Trefor's van.

Johnny shrugged. 'It could be that he is out at his family's Hendre Baili Farm. I noticed the front door was closed as we turned in, mind.'

'That is not a good sign.' Alan said. 'C'mon, let's see if he's in anyway.' Leading the way around the building, he lightly touched the front door with the palm of his hand and it swung easily inwards. He grinned, looking over his shoulder at the same time as he said, 'The bluddy door stop had moved, that's all. C'mon. Let's tell 'im what we've seen and go from there.'

'Well, what *you've* seen, Al. I didn't notice it – I was too busy watching the road,' said Johnny.

Entering the bar, they found they were the only customers there, as it was still so early. Trefor, who was polishing a pint glass until it sparkled like crystal, looked around with a broad smile. 'Hello, boys! How are things with you two?'

'Things are going pretty good for us, Tref.' Alan paused momentarily, then went on. 'Tell me, where's that little van of yours, then?'

Puzzled, Trefor looked from one to the other, then replied 'It's out the back where it always is. Why do you ask, Alan?'

Alan sucked in a deep breath and then said, 'Because we think it's in the ditch over by the chapel!'

'Never! You boys are just having me on, aren't you?'

'No, we're not, Tref,' Johnny cut in. 'Seeing is believing and you need to see for yourself, if you don't believe us. Alan saw it, I didn't. C'mon, let's go outside to see if it's there or not then.'

Trefor looked at each of them in turn and began grinning. 'No, you don't. You two jokers aren't going to catch me out like that.'

Johnny raised his shoulders, hands spread out. 'We're serious, Tref. Honest to God, this is no joke.

'I've got a better idea,' Trefor replied. 'I'll get my car keys to show you, right away.' He ducked under the counter without opening the hatch door, to go into his kitchen across the hallway. Moments later he ducked back into the bar, with a shocked look on his usually placid features.

'Boys, would you believe it? My bluddy keys 'ave gone from the kitchen table where I left them. Now then! That bluddy Ned Pant-y-waun is the only one who's been in yere today. He came in yere a while ago to have a cup of tea with me. He said he was going to catch the next bus to Waun-gron. The bluddy cheeky sod must taken them off the kitchen table, from where I left them this morning when I came back from Hendre Baili. Now what in the world can I do?'

'Well, first of all you need to find out for sure if the van over there is yours. Although Alan's pretty sure it is, Tref,' Johnny said earnestly. 'We can take you there right away and bring you back if it isn't. Just lock up, and we can be there and back in no time at all. Right, Al?'

'Okay by me! C'mon then, let's go!'

Alan leading the way, they sat in the Jag to wait for Trefor. He came around the corner struggling to get his coat on because of the high wind, and hurriedly climbed into the back of the car.

With Alan now driving because he knew exactly where the van was, not a word was spoken for the couple of minutes it took to arrive where the headlights once again picked out the van, tilted into the shallow ditch by the chapel.

'That's my bluddy van!' Trefor shouted, almost deafening them in the front seats. The Jag came to an abrupt stop as he tried to open the door while the car was still moving. 'Wait till I catch hold of 'im!' he shouted. 'I'll give him a bluddy biff, that's what I'll do!'

'That's not a good idea, Tref,' Johnny cautioned him. 'Knowing Ned as we do, he'll have you in court for assault. Much better to call the police and have him charged with taking it without your permission.'

44

Trefor stood with hands on hips as he said, 'And where will we find a bluddy policeman at this time of the day?'

'I'll take you down to Waun-gron right away,' Alan replied. 'We're not doing anything in particular at the moment, are we, Johnny?'

'Not a thing, Al,' he replied.

'C'mon, Tref. Let's go and get the police and then we'll help you to get your van out of there. Are the keys still in there?'

'Yes, but the bluddy doors are locked. Damn it all! What a potch! All because of that Ned Pant-y-waun.' He looked at them, his face like thunder and his meaty fists bunched ready to dish out a punch or two.

'Aye,' said Johnny, 'I know just how you feel, Trefor, but the police are the best option. Hey, wait a minute, we don't have to go far to call the police, there's a call box just back up there on the main road. Alan, you take Trefor up there and I'll stay by yere with the van, just in case Ned comes back.'

Five then ten minutes passed with no sign of the culprit, then Alan and Trefor returned. Trefor's features were still like thunder as he said gruffly, 'The police said they'll be up yere right away from Aberdare. The policeman on duty in Waun-gron was on his own, so he relayed my complaint to the main station there. Damn that Ned! Sorry, boys! I thank you very much for all your help today with this nonsense!'

At that moment the dark blue police van pulled up alongside Alan's car and two hefty constables climbed out. One of them, who knew Trefor, tried his best not to smile.

'Well, yere we are boys. The van is locked, is it?'

'Unfortunately, yes, it is,' Trefor waved his hands despairingly.

'Not a problem, Trefor,' Constable George Jones went back to the van and came back with a thin, flat piece of spring steel about three feet long that had a small notch at the bottom of it. He slid it down into the door between the glass and the rubber seal. There was an audible click and he opened the driver's door.

'There we are, Trefor: just like magic, innit?'

Trefor was all smiles in an instant. 'Thank you, Constable Jones. That was very clever.'

'All part of the service, Trefor. Now, there's no point in looking for fingerprints, because you know very well who the man is who took your vehicle! Is that correct?'

'Oh, indeed! I know exactly who the bluddy culprit is and I want him charged with theft of my keys from my kitchen table when my back was turned, and also with stealing my van. This is my van!' He pointed to the vehicle beside him.

'Righto, Mr. Williams, we can do that, but first we need to get it out of the ditch. Right, boys?' He looked at Johnny and Alan for support.

Nodding their heads as one, they stepped forward and each gripped a door jamb after Trefor had lowered the windows. With one of the constables watching for any approaching traffic and the other pushing for all he was worth on the bonnet of the van, it only took one concerted effort and Trefor's van was back on four wheels.

Constable George Jones stood upright and held his back momentarily. 'Right then, Trefor: start it up and make sure it's in running order and then we'll follow you to the Plough to take your statement of the facts as you know them.' He turned towards Alan and Johnny and said, 'I would like to thank you two lads for your assistance in all this.' He then reached out to shake each of them by the hand.

Johnny nodded and then, addressing Trefor, he said, 'We'll see you later tonight, Tref, so you can give us all the *clecs*.'

CHAPTER 7

Ned Pant-y-waun

WHEN ALAN AND Johnny entered the main room in the Plough Inn about an hour before closing time, they found two pints of best bitter waiting for them on the bar.

Trefor, his round features wreathed in smiles, was there to greet them and shake them by the hand with grateful thanks for their earlier assistance.

'What's new then, Trefor, on the Ned Pant-y-waun saga? Have the cops caught the rotter yet?'

'Not yet, Alan. Not as far as I know, anyway; but it's only a matter of time. I called the police station now just and they told me they had already been to Pant-y-waun Farm but he was nowhere in sight. His sister told them to look for him in some of his usual haunts.'

'His sister told them that?' Johnny's tone was incredulous.

'Oh yes. She's very religious, mind, and won't stand for any old nonsense from Ned.'

'Oh! To change the subject, Tref: how are things with your butcher friend now? Is he still being a nuisance for you?'

'Oh yes. As a matter of fact, he – I'm sure it was him – called me again at three o'clock this morning. I still can't understand why he does it. He must be deliberately waiting up or getting out of bed to do this. It's more than a bit *twp* when you stop and think about it, isn't it?'

Johnny smiled. 'Aye, you're right enough, Tref; but in this world it takes all sorts, mind. I remember working for a foreman who got really annoyed when a couple of blokes came back from lunch break just a couple of minutes late. It was only two minutes, if that. In that machine shop we were all on piecework so that bit of time didn't really matter anyway because we were all chasing the clock all day. Anyway, this foreman decided to put a lock on the clock so we couldn't punch back in early. Which meant *he* had to be there to unlock the clock about two minutes before clocking in time! I told him he was wasting his own lunch hour just because of two blokes. It would have been so much easier to give those two blokes a right bollocking instead of penalising everyone else. He wouldn't have it, and that bluddy butcher is just the same. *Twp* as 'ell.'

'Aaah. Don't you worry your heads about it, boys! I'll just keep on catching him out at every chance I get. I know it drives him mad each time but as long as he doesn't come in yere, I don't care.'

As Alan, Johnny and Trefor were quietly discussing a few other local issues at the far end of the bar, Old John Shinkins, seeing this, made his way to the bar, empty glass in hand, and banged it loudly on the mahogany top to draw their attention to his needs.

'Pint please, Trefor.' He looked towards the two councillors and winked broadly at the same time, saying in a loud whisper, 'I've yerd a few stories about Ned Pant-y-waun. Is there any truth in what I've yerd, Tref?' He looked again at the other two as if for confirmation and winked again.

'Well, John *bach*. How can I answer that when I have no idea what stories or whispers you've yerd or what you are talking about – isn't that right, boys?' he replied, nodding to them while pulling a pint for Old John.

Old John Shinkins stood back a pace from the bar as he said,

'C'mon, Trefor. You can spill the beans to us few by yere. It will be in the *Aberdare Leader* soon enough, won't it?'

'John *bach*, I don't know anything yet! Just wait and see, just like me, is it?'

Two nights later the news of Ned Pant-y-waun's arrest was big news all over the place. It appeared the police had caught up with him, drinking on his own, in a back room of the Croesbychan pub on the old road to Merthyr. Apparently, the landlord there had told them that, to his certain knowledge, 'This man has never been in yere before'.

Old John Shinkins was the first one into the Plough that night and as he entered the bar, he called out, 'Right then, Tref! A pint first and then the story about Ned Pant-y-waun.'

Trefor smiled. 'John *bach*. I'm sure that you know as much, if not more than I know about his nonsense! Tell you what: you tell me what you've yerd so far and I'll confirm if it's true.' He placed the foaming pint on the bar but didn't ask for payment.

Old John looked from the pint to Trefor and back to the pint without saying a word. He then raised the glass and took a swig, smacking his lips in satisfaction. 'Right then: I yerd Ned was in yere a few days ago and he stole your van behind your back!' He looked challengingly at the landlord over the rim of his glass.

'Now, that part is true, John.'

'And he had a crash in it, so I've been told.'

'Not quite a crash, John, but close enough. Go on, then!'

'And I yerd that you reported 'im to the police and had 'im arrested.'

'John *bach*, listen. I reported my van had been stolen from out the back, where I always park it. I also told the police that it was possible that Ned was the one responsible for taking it. I am sure that the police will be doing their job in looking for him. I did hear that they had spoken to him in the Croesbychan pub the other night. Since then, I have no idea what is going on with Ned – and now you know as much as I do about it. Fair enough?

'Yes, boys?' Trefor turned his attention to the two councillors, who had just entered the room. He was glad of this distraction to get away from Old John's interrogation tactics.

'Two pints of best bitter, please, Tref.' Johnny's money was on the bar a split second before Alan's hand came out of his pocket.

Old John smiled at them, then said, 'We were just discussing Ned Pant-y-waun and his old nonsense with Trefor's van.'

'Ned Pant-y-waun! *Peidiwch sôn!*' Johnny replied. 'I was speaking to my aunty down in Waun-gron last night and I just happened to mention Ned's name. I only said it because his sister used to clean for her once a week. Hah! She went off top like a stick of dynamite in temper at the very mention of that man's name.' Johnny immediately had everyone's attention.

'Well, don't stop now, Johnny. Go on,' Trefor stopped polishing the glass he was holding, directing all his attention at the narrator and waiting for the rest of the story.

'Well, it turned out that Ned had called into my aunty's house for cup of tea and a chat. As he had done with you, Tref. And then, when someone had come to the front door and her back was turned, he had stolen some money from her purse. She told me that when she came back, he finished up that hot cup of tea a bit sharpish and skelped it out of there to catch the Red and White bus to Aberdare.

'Only when the paperboy came for his money did she notice that a £5 note had gone from her purse. She bluddy had him later though. She went out to meet every bus coming back up the valley, looking for him. She finally saw him on the very last bus. You know my aunty – she's a pretty big woman, right, Tref?'

'Oh aye,' Trefor agreed, with a chuckle, putting the polished glass under the bar. 'She's not a woman you would want to have a squabble with, I'll say that about her.'

Johnny nodded and went on. 'That Ned is nothing more than a little pilk and he didn't stand a chance once she caught hold of him. She told me the bus was crowded but she had spotted him sitting right at the back. So, she said "Excuse me" to everyone, and got on the bus after telling everyone she was after a thief who had stolen money from her purse. She said she grabbed him by the scruff and dragged him off the bus with everyone cheering for her. She said they cheered even more when she shook him and accused him of stealing a £5 note from her purse. I would have loved to have been there to see that. Well, she had him off the bus and started knocking him about, asking for her money back, but the rotten sod had spent it all on beer or something so there was no money to be had. She told me that while all this was happening, the crowd cheered and stood back to give her room! Even the Red and White bus driver waited to see what was happening. In the end she dragged Ned around the corner and told him if he ever came near her house again, she would give him another leathering that he would remember for the rest of his life.

'Since that was the last bus up the valley, the little thief had to walk home. Good enough for the little sod.'

Old John started laughing and touched Johnny on his arm. 'I've known your aunty for many, many years and boys, she's got a temper mind. You just don't want to cross anyone from that family. Fair play, they are all as good as gold but any of them can go off just like a match.'

Alan patted his brother-in-law on his broad shoulder. 'And I know all about that Wills temper, don't I, Johnny?'

Johnny, his dark eyes flashing momentarily, merely grinned and said, 'Well, you all know how it is, boys. And no, she didn't call the police. She thought that giving him a real good hiding was enough.'

CHAPTER 8

Trefor's Black Eye

A LITTLE OVER a week had passed uneventfully in the Plough's fraternity when Johnny and Alan sauntered into the main bar. Trefor had his back to them when he heard their distinctive voices and called out, 'Hello boys, how's things then?' – but without turning around to face them. Johnny, slightly puzzled, looked at Alan, who just shrugged.

'So, what's up with you then, Tref?' Johnny walked slowly towards him.

Trefor turned to face them, sporting a huge black eye and a swollen, heavily bruised cheek.

'What the 'ell happened to you then, Trefor? Did you fall, or walk into a door or something?'

'No, boys! Nothing as simple as that. It was that bluddy Ned Pant-y-waun again. I was down in Waun-gron standing on the road bridge by the Globe Inn – you know the place. I was looking towards those two yuge blocks of flats and I was thinking how out of place they looked in Waun-gron. Suddenly I felt this tremendous bang on the side of my face. That bluddy Ned Pant-y-waun had sneaked up behind me and punched me on the side of my face. He hit me so hard, my new hat flew off and went over the wall into the river – and I'd only just paid £8 for that, too.'

Johnny had a tough time not to laugh at the seriousness in Trefor's tone about the loss of his new hat. Apparently, his black eye took second place in this event. 'Tell me then, Trefor, did you go to the police and report this personal assault?'

'Yes, I certainly did! Do you blame me for reporting him?'

'Not at all, Trefor!' Johnny and Alan replied together.

'So, when's his court appearance for stealing your van?'

'I think it's next Thursday and I have to be there by ten o'clock,' Trefor replied, pulling a face. 'He's a bluddy fool, isn't he? The constable who came yere to take my statement said Ned didn't have a current driving licence either.'

'Never!' Johnny laughed. 'He'll cop it for that too. I think he'll be very lucky not to follow our friend Bandit to Swansea clink. It sometimes seems Bandit's in and out of there every other week! I'm exaggerating, mind.'

'And after what Ned Pant-y-waun's done to me,' Trefor gingerly touched his face, 'I hope he ends up there for a good spell.'

At the beginning of the following week, Alan and Johnny by a strange coincidence both suffered accidents in work. Johnny had a broken wrist and had his right arm in plaster up to his elbow, and Alan tripped over and broke a bone in his shin.

Trefor looked at them open-mouthed as Johnny held the door open for Alan to hobble through into the bar on crutches.

'What 'ave happened to you two, then? Have you been in a car crash or something?'

Johnny replied, smiling. 'Nothing as horrible as that, Tref. Just a couple of silly accidents in work. Alan's happened on Monday and mine happened about six weeks ago! I had a bit of a bump getting down off my machine and didn't think much of it. Not until I found I couldn't move it in a certain way. So, I went down to Waun-gron the other day and saw a doctor. He sent me for an X-ray and told me I had a broken wrist.' He banged the heavy plaster cast on the bar and said with a laugh, 'Two pints please, Mister Landlord!'

Trefor was pulling the first pint when a thought struck him. 'So how did you boys get yere tonight then? I'm pretty sure you didn't walk yere from the Bryn, did you?'

Johnny and Alan laughed at the same time and Alan replied, 'No, by damn, Trefor! We drove yere in my car. Johnny looks after the steering wheel and the pedals and I change the gears when he tells me to. With a bit of practice, we're managing all right.' Then, after a pause, he added, 'Up to now, that is.'

Trefor, his eyebrows raised in question, asked, 'Isn't that against the law, Johnny, driving a vehicle between you like that?'

'Could very well be,' Johnny replied. 'But who's going to know that when we're doing a mile a minute, eh?'

'Well, you be careful, boys. We don't want the police calling in yere anymore.'

Colin looked up when they came over to the big farmhouse table with their drinks, and laughed out loud. 'You two are like a pair of bluddy cripples about the place! By damn, Alf came in earlier with 'is arm in a sling and now you two! This place looks more like a bluddy doctor's surgery than a pub!'

'That's as maybe,' Alan replied, 'but we're still clever enough to beat you at crib.' And with that he leaned forward and rapped hard with his knuckles on the table as a challenge to Colin and Bobby, his usual playing partner.

Once on the card table, Alan and Johnny were having a good run of luck playing as partners in the game of four-handed crib. This was the fifth game in a row they had won for a pint a corner. Johnny looked at the two full pint glasses at his elbow, both as yet untouched, and the one he was already drinking from. He called out to Trefor, 'Hey, Tref! These two pints I've already got yere are in danger of going flat. If we win this game, don't pull another pint for me – just leave it over the bar, please.'

'Same for me too, Tref!' Alan smiled at his brother-in-law. 'Yere's hoping we lose this one, *brawd*.'

'Right enough, Al. Colin, can I ask you again to shuffle and deal for me? This damn plaster cast is a nuisance – and I got a telling off from the emergency ward Sister at the hospital yesterday after I accidentally went swimming in Caswell Bay.'

Alan looked at the scoreboard. 'I don't think so, Johnny. I'm holding a dozen and we only need ten holes to peg out. I don't know about you, but I think I've had enough cards for tonight. Besides, I've got this pint to finish and two by yere, as well as another one over the bar now.'

'Okay by me.' Johnny stood up, holding his back. 'Yere you are, boys. We're off the table. As winners,' he added, smiling. 'Yere, Colin, have one of these pints and thanks for dealing for me.'

'What's that you were saying about Caswell Bay, Johnny?' asked Trefor, from the bar.

'Aye, come on, Johnny!' Old John Shinkins was standing at the end of the bar neearest the table, waiting to be served. 'It's no good tellin' half a bluddy story, mun.'

'Okay, Mr Shinkins. As I was going to say before I got distracted, I went down to Caswell for a jaunt out. It was pretty awkward trying to drive, mind, because I couldn't hold the steering wheel when I shifted gears, but I took my time. Anyway, I thought I could go in for a dip, holding my plaster cast above my head and wading in up to my waist – that was, until an extra big wave nearly swamped me and the bluddy plaster got soaked through. So I thought, what the 'ell, and tried to swim – and every second stroke sounded like a loud "paloosh" as the plaster hit the water. It ended up as soggy as 'ell and that's why I got the telling off at the hospital!'

He stood up and picked his way carefully through the other patrons, carrying his pint to the far end of the bar, then went back twice to carry Alan's beers and place them alongside his own full pint. He puffed out his cheeks and said, 'Der, Tref! We haven't had a run of luck like that for a very long time.'

'Sometimes it's much better to be lucky than rich.' Trefor smiled as he dried some glasses.

'Oh, I don't know,' Alan said, hobbling up to the bar on his crutches. 'I wouldn't mind being just half a crown behind your bank account any day of the week.'

Trefor smiled. 'That's very kind of you, Alan, to portray me as a rich man. If only it was true!'

'Der, Tref, you should have seen us the other night! My wife said it would be nice to have a real Christmas tree this year for a change, instead of that old artificial one that's falling to bits. Then my brother-in-law, old clever clogs yere, said we can easily get a real one from up in the Forestry. There's millions of them up on Craig y Llyn mountain. Me, like a clown, says, "Aye, okay, let's go and get one, then." Can you imagine it, boys? Me with my leg in plaster and him with his arm – his right arm, mind – in plaster, up on the mountain in pitch black, searching for a tidy little Christmas tree! Well, we somehow managed to get up there, close by the gate into the Forestry, then we found it was locked. Then my brother-in-law… go on, Johnny, you tell the rest of the story.'

'Aye, okay. Well, boys, in the lights from a passing car, I caught a glimpse of a small tree outside the Forestry fence, so I said to Alan, "Don't bother about going in there. There's one right by yere that looks okay." I'll tell you, boys, we had a lot of potch cutting that one down. All Alan could do was to stand there on one leg holding the top of the tree while I was struggling to use a hacksaw in my left hand, and I couldn't hold onto anything. Only my fingertips were sticking out of the plaster cast, just as you can see now. Well, we got it cut down in the end, ducking down every time a car went past, and brought it back to Alan's house. Once we had it inside, we could see that there were hardly any branches on one side of it and we had a bluddy good laugh at ourselves after all the potch we went through to get it. It felt like we had been out on Craig y Llyn mountain for hours and had nothing to show for it.

'My sister, who was a bit cleverer than us at the time, told us to trim those few branches from that side and put it flat against the wall. So that's what we did, and it looks tidy too. Right, Alan?'

Alan and Johnny joined in the laughter following the tale of the Christmas tree, then – their beer finished – they left the smoke-filled bar to make their way home.

Thursday arrived, when Ned Pant-y-waun was to appear at the Magistrates Court in Aberdare. Trefor, being the plaintiff, was to appear for the prosecution in the case of his stolen van. Alan and Johnny, as good as their word, sat near the front of the court, just in case they were called as material witnesses to the alleged crime.

Ned Pant-y-waun was sitting off to one side with the court-appointed solicitor at his side.

At exactly nine o'clock the Clerk of the Court read the charges of taking Mr Trefor Williams' van without permission and of driving without a driving licence or insurance. Ned was asked, 'How do you plead?'

At the prompting of his solicitor, Ned stood up and pleaded in a loud voice, 'Not guilty, sir,' then sat down, glaring balefully at his accuser, Trefor, across the room.

Trefor stared, open-mouthed, at Ned's audacity. He turned to Johnny and Alan and said in a shocked tone, 'What do you think of that, boys? The gall of the man to say that!'

Johnny leaned forward and whispered, 'Well, Tref. You didn't *catch* him stealing your van and the police never took any fingerprints either, did they? So, you never know, mind!'

'He bluddy took it, boys, cos he was the only one who came into my kitchen. Oh, the lying sod – that he is!'

The Clerk of the Court stood up and called out, 'Is the plaintiff, Mr Trefor Williams, Plough Inn, Rhyd-y-groes, present?'

Trefor, resplendent in his Sunday-best pinstripe suit, rose from his seat and replied, 'I am yere, sir.'

The Clerk nodded, shuffled some papers in his hands and asked Trefor to enter the witness box, then asked him to place his hand on the Bible and swear to tell the truth, the whole truth and nothing but the truth in any statement he made. He did as requested and turned to face the Bench.

The Chairman looked hard at him. 'My goodness, Mr Williams, you appear to have been in the wars. Pray tell us, what happened to your face?'

Trefor briefly touched his still-swollen cheek and a black eye that had all the colours of the rainbow radiating from the massive bruise.

'Well, sir, just over a week ago I was standing on a bridge by the Globe Inn in Waun-gron and admiring those two magnificent edifices built by the council when the defendant, Ned Pant-y-waun, came up behind me and struck me a dastardly blow to the side of my face. He hit me so hard he knocked my brand new hat off, which went over the wall into the river – and I had only just paid £8 for it, too. Then he ran away down High Street towards the Cenotaph before I could do anything about it, sir.'

The Chairman tried to hide his involuntary smile behind his hand as Trefor went on. 'When I had recovered a bit, I followed him down to the Cenotaph, but there was no sign of him. I went into the police station right there and then to report what he…' (Trefor pointed an accusing finger at Ned Pant-y-waun) '…just done to me and the sergeant on duty took my statement and I left. Oh yes! He also said he would be making out a charge of an unprovoked assault against *him*!' He pointed his finger at Ned, and thumped the rail of the witness box with his other fist until it rattled.

'Now, now, Mr Williams. Please calm yourself. I'm sure that case will come before us soon enough, and we will deal with that then. To move on. We would now like to hear your version, as you know it, of the alleged theft of your vehicle on the date given in your statement to the local police. If you please, Mr Williams.'

Trefor straightened up in the witness box and cleared his throat 'Ahem. Well, sir, it was on Wednesday a few weeks ago when he, Ned Pant-y-waun, came into my public house. He didn't want any beer, but said he would enjoy a nice cup of tea and a chat. Since there were no other customers, there being no racing – horse racing that is, sir – and as I have known him for many years, I invited him to join me in my kitchen.

'I made a fresh pot and poured a cup for myself and one for him and then the phone rang. So I got up from my chair to answer it. While my back was turned, that must have been when he picked up my keys off the table – which I realised after, would have been right there in front of him. I recalled later that he had drunk that hot tea pretty quick, and said he was in a rush to catch the bus to Aberdare and left right away. I thought it a bit strange at the time, since he'd said he wanted to have a chat and then didn't. But people can be funny, so I didn't give it another thought, sir.

'It wasn't until much later that two good friends of mine spotted what they thought was my van in a ditch on the other side of the village. They were coming home from Neath and by some coincidence turned into the village from the top end, otherwise I would never have known until the following day, or maybe even longer, sir. They came into my pub and asked me where my van was. I told them it was out the back where I always park it. It was then I went to look for my keys, but couldn't find them anywhere. I went with them outside and there was no sign of my vehicle. My friends kindly offered to drive me over to the place where they thought my van was. As soon as I saw it, I knew right away it was mine! Well, you do, don't you? It was partially in the ditch on the wrong side of the road, with the front wheel on the passenger side in there, and the doors were locked but my keys were still in the ignition. When the police arrived, they opened the doors for me and asked me to start it up. It felt okay, so I drove it back to the Plough and parked it where I always leave it.' He shrugged. 'The police eventually caught the culprit!' He turned and glared at Ned Pant-y-waun. 'And yere we are today, sir.'

'We thank you, Mr Williams, for your very comprehensive and detailed explanation of the events as you know them, leading us up to this point in the proceedings. You may stand down.'

He nodded to the Clerk, who shuffled his papers and called out, 'Constable George Jones. Please enter the witness box.' He held out a Bible for the policeman to swear the oath on, then asked him to proceed with his evidence.

'On that day, as mentioned by Mr Williams, I received a call from the station in Waun-gron outlining his complaint against Ned Davies, Pant-y-waun Farm. The officer advised that he was on his own and would not be able to leave the station at that time.' He opened his notebook and glanced at the closely written notes. 'So, it was decided that Constable Johnstone and myself would travel in our van to the area of Rhyd-y-groes as indicated in the complaint. When we arrived, we found the plaintiff's van in the ditch on the wrong side of the road. Mr Williams appeared very agitated. The vehicle was locked and the keys were inside. I used an item out of our equipment box to release the locked doors.' He again referred to his notebook.

'Between us, Mr Williams and two of his local friends,' he indicated Johnny and Alan in the front of the court with a nod of his head, 'we easily managed to push the van back onto the road without incident. I then advised the plaintiff to start it up and inspect it for any visible damage. At that point, he said there was none that he could see. He drove it back to the Plough

Inn and Constable Johnstone and myself followed him to take his statement of the events leading up to the discovery of the missing van. I have listened carefully to Mr Williams giving his evidence and I can confirm that what he has said today is exactly as my notes show, sir.' He looked up at the Bench and received a nod of approval from the Chairman.

'You may step down, Constable Jones.'

'Thank you, sir,' He stepped out of the witness box with a brief nod and a barely perceptible grin towards Trefor, Johnny and Alan.

The Clerk of the Court again stood up and called out, 'Will the defendant, Ned Davies of Pant-y-waun Farm, take the stand, please?'

After Ned had been sworn in and the summary of the charges against him read out, he was asked by the Chairman, 'How do you plead against these charges, Mr Davies?'

In a truculent tone of voice, he said brazenly, 'Not guilty!'

Trefor, sitting alongside Johnny and Alan, jumped to his feet, a look of anger on his round features at Ned's response. He opened his mouth as if to say something, but Johnny reached out to touch his arm and silently mouthed NO. Trefor sat back down quickly, bunching his meaty fists, as he glared at Ned Pant-y-waun.

The Chairman looked down at Ned over his gold-rimmed half-moon spectacles. 'The evidence against you, Mr Davies, although it's circumstantial, is pretty damning, isn't it? You are the only one who was there, in his kitchen, who had the opportunity to commit this offence and take Mr Williams' keys, without his knowledge, which gave you access to his vehicle. Isn't that so?'

Ned, his head bowed, started to nod agreement, then stopped suddenly, as if realising he was unwittingly admitting his guilt to everyone in the room.

'And it is also clear that you possess neither a driving licence nor the relevant insurance to drive any vehicle,' the Chairman went on. 'By virtue of your actions, you must also realise that these offences carry a custodial sentence. Therefore, Mr Davies, we find you guilty as charged and sentence you to 14 days in Her Majesty's Prison in Swansea. You will also be fined £100 and court costs. Bailiff! Take him from here, please.

As Ned was being led away, the Clerk of the Court approached the Bench with a sheaf of papers in his hand. Moments later the Chairman motioned the Court Bailiff to return Ned Pant-y-waun to the dock.

'It appears, Mr Davies, that your charge of assault on Mr Williams, the Plough Inn, Rhyd-y-groes, is also before this Court today. How do you plead?'

He glared balefully at his accuser and in an almost angry tone replied, 'Not guilty!'

'Hmm.' The Chairman glanced at the single sheet of paper in his hand and passed it in turn to the two other Justices.

'You say "not guilty", Mr Davies, but I have in my hand an affidavit from a member of this Court who witnessed your assault on Mr Williams in Waun-gron. What do you have to say to that? Not very much, I imagine.' He conferred briefly with his colleagues and said dryly, 'We find you guilty as charged and fine you a further £100 plus court costs. Bailiff, take him away.'

As Ned Pant-y-waun was led away, he looked back over his shoulder and glared at Trefor with malice in his beady eyes, mouthing silently, 'I'll have you, Trefor Plough.'

'Did you see that, boys?' asked Trefor, shocked.

'Aye, we did. I think you'll have to watch out for him when he gets out.' Johnny gave a short laugh.

With three sets of eyes following Ned's retreating back, Alan said softly. 'You know, all of this today is his own fault, so why should he threaten you, Tref?'

Trefor shrugged. 'I have no idea, boys, but never mind him now. I'll just have to watch out for him when he gets out, that's all. It will make me feel a little bit safer if I know that you boys will be watching for him too.'

'No problem, Tref,' Johnny replied, as his brother-in-law nodded in agreement.

CHAPTER 9

Old John

WHEN ALAN AND Johnny eased their way into the main bar on the evening after Trefor's day in court, Old John Shinkins appeared delighted to see them. He was seated in his usual place on the wooden settle beside the stove. He stood up and smiled as he greeted them, gesturing to them to come over to him. Johnny, walking behind his brother-in-law, gave him a nudge and murmured quietly, 'Uh-oh! He wants something from us, Al. Careful what you say.' Aloud, he said, 'Mr Shinkins! How are you this fine evening?'

Old John, a broad smile on his weathered features, replied, 'I am doing pretty good, boys, but I have a question for you both. Did you go to the court in Aberdare yesterday about Trefor's little van?'

'Now why in the world would you want to know about that, then?' Johnny half-turned to wink at his brother-in-law.

'Well, because I have tried my best to get some information out of Trefor over there,' he nodded towards the landlord, who knew in an instant that he was being discussed. 'But he wouldn't let on. Not one bit. I've kept on to 'im, but all he did was smile and then he gave me a free pint to stop pestering 'im.'

'So you took the free pint, then!'

'Well, of course I did. Trefor doesn't give too many free pints away, does he?'

'And now, Mr Shinkins, you want to know all the *clecs* from us. Is that it?'

'Well, of course I do. If you don't mind, that is. You don't mind, do you, boys?'

'Well, now then, let's get this straight, is it? If Trefor doesn't want you to know anything about it, how can we go against his wishes?' Alan turned towards Johnny, tongue in cheek.

'Aww. C'mon, boys! I've been waiting on pins all night for you to come in and now you won't let on. Be fair, boys, it will be in the *Aberdare Leader* next week but I don't want to wait that long, do I?'

'Tell you what, then. Let us have time for a couple of pints first and then you come over to where we always are at the far end of the bar. Where Trefor is right now, polishing glasses. You know he's watching us, don't you? He'll know exactly what you've been speaking to us about as well, won't he?'

Old John turned to look across the room at Trefor, who just smiled knowingly back at him.

'Aye, all right, but remember my patience will only last for so long, mind.'

Johnny and Alan continued their slow progress towards the bar, stopping to chat here and there to friends in the crowd until they arrived at the spot where Trefor had already placed a pint of best bitter for each of them. He smiled in welcome and murmured in soft tones, 'I noticed that Old John buttonholed you boys from the moment you came through the door. He wanted to know from me what happened in the court in Aberdare yesterday, too, but I was pretty busy so I gave him a pint for free just to leave me alone.'

'Aye. He told us that too. That must be a first for him to stop pestering. No wonder he's a bit excitable tonight.'

'It is, but I wanted a bit of peace and quiet after yesterday's nonsense with Ned Pant-y-waun.'

'Well, your eye is looking a lot better and the colours are a lot prettier, almost matching the colours of your jersey now.'

Trefor laughed. 'You're right enough, Alan.' He looked down at the variety of knitted patches sewn onto his ancient jersey. 'I think I've got all the colours of the rainbow, haven't I? Seriously boys, that Ned is a bad egg, all right. I still can't understand why he did it in the first place! Can you?'

'We don't know him all that well, Tref, so it's hard to judge what he might be capable of doing in the right situation. Temptation can do funny things to a person's mind. Personally, I think he is a very sly person. He has that look about him, and I think you are going to need your wits about you when he gets out of Swansea clink.

'Hey, Tref, to get back to Old John. We told him to give us time to have a couple of pints and then to come over by yere for a chat. Is that okay by you?'

'Oh yes, that's okay. Another two pints, is it?'

'I'm buying!' Alan stepped forward quickly to pay before Johnny could even move an inch.

Trefor grinned. 'I don't know about you two. You're always trying to beat the other to the punch when it comes to paying first. I don't mind who it is, so long as I get paid!'

Alan lifted his foaming pint and looked across the room over the rim of the glass. He could see that Old John was preparing to get up from his seat, all the while watching Johnny and Trefor sharing some sort of joke as they held their sides laughing.

Alan carefully placed his pint on the bar and said, 'Boys, he's watching us and he's already in his starting blocks to make his move in this direction!'

Trefor and Johnny looked up and saw Old John pushing his way between the tables towards them. He leaned on the edge of the bar, slightly out of breath, evidence enough of the many years he had spent working in the dust-filled environment underground in the local coal mines. He gave himself a slight thump on the front of his chest using the side of his fist. 'This old dust gets me sometimes,' he said, by way of explanation. 'Right then, boys! Let's have it, then! I want to know what happened with Ned Pant-y-waun in Aberdare Court yesterday.' He looked from one to the other, smiling broadly as he did so.

Trefor put down the glass he was holding and placed his hands flat on the bar. 'Well, John *bach*. He got exactly what he deserved. Fourteen days in the Swansea "Crowbar Hotel" for taking my little van without permission and driving it without a driving licence or insurance. He was also fined £100 for that, and another £100 for hitting me in the face.'

'*Duw, Duw!* That's a lot, innit? Mind you, I think he can be a really nasty chap when he has a mind to be.' He looked closely at Trefor's eye. 'I'll say this, though, the colours around your eye are almost matching the colours on your jumper.'

Trefor laughed, with the others joining in. 'Alan said the same thing just a few minutes ago, John, but it doesn't bother me now. It did in the beginning, mind, with everyone poking fun or wanting to know what happened, until I got a bit fed up explaining umpteen times a day. Now I don't care.' He pulled at the front of his old jersey. 'I don't care if people poke fun at this either, John. It keeps me warm.'

Old John reached out to shake Trefor by the hand and, nodding his head, he said, 'That Ned will be off top about the sentence. What a bluddy *twpsyn*.'

'Well, it was his own bluddy fault, isn't it?' Trefor turned away to serve another customer.

Johnny, smiling at Old John, said, 'Now you've had all the *clecs* as we know them.'

'Aye, indeed. What a shambles to get into, though, isn't it?'

Colin came up to the bar at that moment and Johnny

tapped him on the shoulder and said, 'I yerd another funny story about your dad last week. The headmistress of the junior school in Waun-gron went on to him after he'd had his name in the *Aberdare Leader* again. She'd known your father for years, mind. This was relating to his exploits with the foxes and cubs he had caught over the past year and about the old tame fox he sold Jack Honeyman. So she said to Fred that the next time he caught any cubs, she thought it might be a good idea if he could bring one to her school so that she could show the little kids what a wild fox cub looked like. Well, he agreed to do just that.'

'Aye, that sounds just like the old man. He was pretty good like that,' Colin replied.

'Wait a minute 'til I tell you the rest of it, Col. It appeared that Fred had been having more than a few drinks when he found a fox cub in one of his snares and remembered her request. The next morning he showed up at the school with the cub. She told me she was shocked when he pulled it from his pocket and put it on her desk – it was already dead! He was 'ell of a boy, Col!'

'That he was, God rest 'im.'

All those standing near Colin and Johnny at the bar laughed out loud at the story.

Trefor chipped in, laughing, 'I don't know about that Jack Honeyman, but wherever he is, he still owes me some money for me allowing him to drink on strap. Then he disappears into the blue yonder!'

'More fool you, Tref, for giving it to him in the first place,' said Alan.

'Oh, I'm not worried one little bit over that money, Alan. I'm sure I will get it all back one day – perhaps with a little bit of interest too. There are times when you just have to have a bit of faith in people.'

'He's right enough, Al. Jack isn't a bad sort – a bit erratic at times, but he's a good worker and when he's flush, everybody around him will get a share of the good times.'

By coincidence, the following week Jack Honeyman knocked on Johnny's door. After greeting each other like long-lost souls, they both settled down in easy chairs to catch up with the intervening years that had passed since the day Jack had so swiftly departed from the village.

'So where did you end up, then? I did know you'd gone for a job interview up in Hereford, and then what?'

'Well, that job lasted a few years and then I got restless again...'

'Again? You're always bluddy restless, mate. Anyway, go on.'

'Well, then I applied for a job out in Africa, and landed it. In fact, it was in Liberia. I was the top dog, looking after all the electrics at a large mill.'

'Hell's bells, Jack. That's quite a jump from Hereford!'

'Well, that job was okay for a while – that is, until the rebels out there took a dislike to their president and the shooting started. I even bought myself a 9 mm automatic pistol. Just for my own protection, mind. When the fighting got much too close to my house, I decided it was time to beat a hasty retreat. That's how I ended up back in London. I've got a little one-bedroom flat, which costs a small fortune in rent but it will do for now.'

'Until you decide to fly off somewhere else, is it?'

Jack grinned but didn't bite on Johnny's probing question. Instead he said, 'Hey, what about going up to have a swift pint in the Plough. Are you in?'

'Aye, okay.' Johnny rose from his seat and stretched, his arms above his head. 'Hey, Jack, do you remember that fox cub you bought off Fred Howells as a pet for your kids? Remember, it had a sort of broken tail. It caused all sorts of trouble around yere a few years back. It killed Old Jack Thomas' chickens and four of his ducks right in front of him!'

'Oh, yes. I remember that bluddy animal. Yes, I do, and that bluddy Fred caught me on that, too. I paid him five quid for it and it was nowhere near as tame as he claimed it was. I kept it in the house for quite a while and the very first time I went to stroke it, the bluddy thing bit me.'

'I know,' Johnny agreed ruefully. 'One day, if you can recall, I was in your house and it looked like it was intending to bite one of your kids. I put my hand out to stop it and it bit me too. C'mon, let's go and see Trefor. I'll bet anything he'll be pleased to see you, mate.'

'I bet he will, too,' Jack replied, grinning. 'I still owe him about four quid since before I went to Hereford. Yes, he'll be pleased to see me, all right.'

The moment they stepped into the main bar, Trefor looked up and said in a loud voice, 'Well, well, the prodigal has returned – and he is just the man I've been waiting to see!'

Jack, all smiles, reached over the bar to shake Trefor's meaty outstretched hand. 'Hello, Trefor. I think I still owe you some money! Sorry about the delay.'

'Yes, you do indeed, Mr Honeyman. You do indeed!'

Jack handed him a crisp £5 note and Trefor crackled it in his fingers and walked towards the till. Lifting the till, he reached under it and handed Jack a crumpled 10 shilling note as he said, 'And yere is your change, sir. Two pints of best bitter, is it?'

Johnny gave Jack a slight nudge. 'I suppose you do know that those old paper notes are no longer legal tender, don't you? You've been out of the country far too long, mate!'

'No, I didn't know that – but it doesn't matter one little bit. The interest alone on what I owed him will no doubt be much more than that.'

'Well, you could take it to any bank and they will change it for you.'

'Not worth the potch, Johnny.'

'Hey, Trefor. I was just talking to Jack before we came in about that "tame" fox he bought off old Fred.'

'Oh, aye! That was a few years back, mind. Fred and Old Jack Thomas had one 'ell of a row in yere over that so-called "tame" animal. It killed almost all of Old Jack's chickens and ducks too. Jack then went after Fred with his walking stick, and almost copped him with it too! It was touch and go in yere for a while. In the end, Fred said to Jack he was going to get your address for him and he could take it up with you for payment for his birds.'

Jack laughed out loud. 'He would have had a hell of a time trying to catch up with me, Tref! I must have been somewhere in West Africa at the time all this happened.'

'West Africa, eh? You must have done a lot of travelling since you left yere.'

'I guess I've done my share and more. For a small village, we've contributed a lot of world travellers. I can think of at least a dozen right off the top of my head...'

'Aye, aye, that's quite a lot,' Old John cut in. 'Never mind the world travellers, what about all those who moved from yere to other parts of Britain, like Bristol and Birmingham and London and such places?'

Colin, standing next to him, empty glass in hand, laughed. 'What do you think this place is, then, Mr Shinkins? A travel agency, or what?'

'No, no. I'm only saying, that's all.'

Jack, finishing his pint, pulled a roll of money from his pocket. 'Trefor: a pint for Johnny, Alan, Colin, Mr Shinkins, Danny over there and a pint each for Twm and Roy – and, oh yes, a pint for Willi Bray too and finally take one for yourself, Tref. I owe you that much.'

'I'll have a scotch then, Mr Honeyman!' So saying, Trefor raised the glass to his lips and wished everyone good health.

CHAPTER 10

Old Jack Thomas

'**O**KAY, TREFOR! WHERE is he, then?'

Trefor looked up, startled, from pulling a fresh pint for Willi Bray. Mouth open, he stared across the crowded room at Old Jack Thomas, who was leaning on his son's arm as he waved his heavy walking cane in the air. His son Danny was trying his best not to laugh as the older man continued to wave his stick, narrowly missing two of the card players sitting at the big table. They had anticipated its trajectory and cwtched down to avoid being hit on their heads or elsewhere by the apparently angry Jack.

Trefor placed the foaming pint on the bar. Straightening up, he enquired, 'May I ask: who are you talking about, Jack Thomas? And be careful with that bluddy stick! I don't want you to hit any of my customers, if you please!'

'I'm talking about that Jack Honeyman, that's who!' His voice still raised, he peered, with eyes squinted, through the crowd, looking for his quarry. 'That bluddy man owes me for fifteen chickens and four ducks his old fox have killed for me!'

'What?!' Trefor started laughing, with some of his customers joining in. 'Jack mun! All that happened more than two years, possibly three years ago!'

'Aye, that's as maybe, Trefor. That bluddy Fred never paid me so I am going after that Jack Honeyman. Where is he, then?'

Johnny stepped forward and, ever mindful of Jack's volatile temper, he said cautiously, 'Well, Mr Thomas. He was yere with me for a little while yesterday but I think he went back to London last night.'

Jack raised his gravelly voice as he swung his stick in the air again and glared in temper around the room. 'Well, I don't care! I want to know where he is up there, cos I'm going after 'im!'

Johnny drew in a deep breath and then went on. 'As far as I remember, Mr Thomas, he said he was living in a small flat.' He paused, trying to remember exactly what he had been told the day before. 'Damn it all, Mr Thomas, I know he said it was in WC something but I can't for the life of me remember what number he said at the time. We were all having a couple of pints, mind, and London is a bluddy big city too! I think there are about eight million people living there, maybe more, right boys?'

There were murmurs of agreement from those at the bar.

'Aye, he's right enough, Dad,' said Danny. 'Boys, I keep on tellin 'im to leave it there but he won't 'ave it. I've told 'im that old fox 'ave probably died of old age by now.'

'I don't care!' His father shouted above the laughter. 'What happened back then was wrong and I want payment for that, just to put things right for me.' He peered around the bar again. 'Are you sure he isn't yere, Trefor? I trust you to tell me the truth, but not this lot.' He waved his stick again to encompass the whole room and narrowly missing a few by a matter of inches.

Trefor began to look alarmed at Jack Thomas' angry attitude and said brightly, 'Never mind him now, Jack. Yere, have a drink on me! Choose any drink you like! Whisky, brandy, best bitter? If I've got it, it's yours. Just say the word! C'mon, have a drink mun, it's free.' The offer appeared to confuse the old man, as he looked from Trefor to the others in a slightly vacant way.

'Consider it a birthday drink, then. How old are you now, then, Jack?'

'I'm ninety...' he paused, trying to recall just how old he was. He turned towards his son. 'How old am I now, then, Danny?'

'Well, Dad. At this very moment I am not too sure, but my missus will know. I'll ask her when we get home, all right?'

Jack grunted something in reply and turned to the bar. 'I'll have a brandy then, Trefor. Can you make it a double? They say that brandy's good for the heart, don't they?'

Trefor's eyebrows raised slightly at Jack's request for a double brandy, but nevertheless he poured it for him and watched with amusement as he swigged it down in one go, to some mild applause from Colin and the others standing at the bar.

'Hey, Trefor,' called Colin. 'You must remember this one about Fred. Me and my father 'ad been 'aving a row – nothing new in that, mind – over the rent for the Mount. I wasn't workin' regular...'

'Nothing new in that either,' Alan chipped in, laughing.

'Aye, Alan, you're right enough there. I wasn't all that fussed to go under, not after my butty got killed with some runaway drams.' He paused momentarily, then went on. 'Anyway, as I was saying: Fred was skint and I only 'ad enough money for one pint and I didn't want to put any more money on strap. Well, we came in yere and my father went straight up to the bar and asked you, Trefor, to lend him a pound...'

'Aye, aye. I remember that now!' said Trefor. 'Fred asked me politely if I could lend him a pound. I was pretty busy at the time so I gave him a pound note. Next thing, he took out his rent book and put the pound note in it and handed it back to me to sign. Damn, he had the nerve of a cat burglar. So, I signed it to show he was up to date with his rent, and gave him the change, which I can't believe I did at the time. Then he turned around and bought himself a pint with MY MONEY!

'Yes, he had a lot of cheek all right, but I still miss the old so and so and his noise in yere. Mind you, he used to come out with such nonsense sometimes it was hard to believe anything he said.'

'Oh, aye. He was full of it, boys!' Colin turned towards the others behind him. 'I remember one time when we were still livin' up in the Bryn, he said he was goin' to old Marc Williams' funeral and I said, "You'll 'ave to dress tidy for that one cos he's 'old village'." He went outside on the street and started shouting: "Who's got a black tie to lend me, and a clean white 'anky?" This shouting went on for a few minutes until, by damn, a couple of women came out of the 'ouses opposite where we lived and would you believe it, one folded a hanky and put it in his top pocket and the other went behind 'im to put the black tie on for 'im! And he just stood there while they tidied 'im up! Aye, he had 'ell of a cheek, all right. He came back into the 'ouse pleased as punch. "There you are," he said, "What did I tell you before, Colin? I'm a legend in my own lifetime and some people are prepared to look after me wherever I go!"

'Aye, and I told 'im what a bluddy cheek he 'ad. He then said, "It's not cheek, Colin. It's because it's me, boy! As I said to you just now, I'm a legend in my own lifetime, aren't I?"

'And boys, if you think about it, he was right! He *was* a bluddy legend, wasn't he? And I am a bit proud of 'im too.' Colin grinned, picked up his pint and moved back to his seat at the card table, with Alan following right on his heels. Alan leaned over the table and rapped hard with his knuckles on the scoreboard, saying at the same time, 'Johnny and me will play the winners, okay?' He stared at the position of the pegs. 'Are those scores correct?'

Colin turned in his seat to look directly at him. 'Of course they're correct! Why are you asking such a *twp* question, Alan?'

'Just joking, boys. Just joking! I was just remembering a story from a long time ago, about an old chap who used to play some cards in yere. Charlie something, his name was.'

Old John Shinkins stood up, empty pint glass in hand. 'I know exactly who you're talking about, Alan. He was a really cantankerous old man. He was quite a bit older than me but I can remember him making a fuss nearly every time he played at this table. Do you know, he was always ready to fight anyone at the drop of a hat over a single point, and he was a pensioner too! He should have had more sense, but there you are. It takes all sorts, I suppose. Yes, he was from Waun-gron originally, same as me. Hey, Trefor! Do you remember Charlie? What was his last name?'

Trefor appeared to be lost in thought for a few moments, then he said, 'No. No, I don't remember what his other name was. I only remember him as Charlie and yes, he could be a bit of a nuisance at times. I remember he always had a butty with him called Twm Harris. He was a quiet chap.'

'Aye, you're right enough, Tref. This Charlie had a little cottage down in Cwm Isaac. Anyway, to get back to what I was going to say about him.'

'Perhaps you'd better sit down again, Mr Shinkins,' Alan advised, holding the older man by the elbow. 'You're looking a little bit shaky holding onto the back of Roy's chair.'

Old John's face broke into a smile. 'Possible you're right there, Alan.'

'Yere, gimme your glass and I'll fill it for you, no charge. I love these stories from years ago.'

Grateful for the respite, Old John returned to his usual spot on the wooden settle. 'Well, as I was saying about Charlie... Damn, I wish I could remember his name. Never mind now. Him and his butty would play anyone for just half a pint a corner and they would always win, no matter who it was they played against. And especially when Charlie did the scoring. As I said, it was always for half a pint and no more than that, until one day a chap from Waun-gron was in yere and he saw how Charlie had his hand all over the scoreboard when he was pegging his and his butty's points. So he sat back and watched how Charlie was able to lift both pegs at the same time and move down the board and pinch a few holes every time. He mentioned this to a few of the boys and that was when they all decided to use three pins whenever Charlie was playing. Of course, he made a bluddy fuss about it and even threatened to knock one boy's block off. Nothing was ever said about his scoring methods, mind, but they didn't win many games after that.' He paused and took a long swig from the pint Alan had brought to him.

'Well, go on, Mr Shinkins. There must be more *clecs* about Charlie whatsisname, isn't there?'

'Aye, there is, boys.' He looked at each of the men gathered around the table and went on.

'This one is a classic, boys. I've already said he was ready to fight anyone at any time of the day. Well, he was a big boxing fan, from the days of bare-fist mountain fighting until today's scraps in the ring. Anyway, there was a world heavyweight fight being held in London at the Harringay Arena and he was determined to go and see it. So, him and his butty Twm Harris decided to go up to London. Somehow, Charlie or his butty managed to get two tickets for the fight, which they showed everybody who wanted to see them. Then, on the day before the big fight, they caught a bus to Waun-gron, then another bus to Aberdare and onto another bus to Cardiff. From there they had a bus to Chepstow, then Reading and finally into London. I think he said it took the best part of fourteen hours, perhaps a bit more. I can't be sure about that – there have been so many stories about their trip, it's hard to know which one to believe.

'Anyway, they got into the Arena after all the other fights were over and the two heavyweights were already stripped off in the ring and ready for the bell to start fighting. That was the moment Charlie turned to argue with the man in the seat behind him and tell him to keep his feet off his seat. He said it took less than a minute but the bell had rung and by the time he had turned around to see what was happening, the fight was over with one of the heavyweights out stone cold in the centre of the ring. He never saw the punch that ended the fight.' Old John started laughing until the tears ran down his weathered cheeks and the others around him in the bar joined in. 'Oh, boys. I can't stop laughing every time I think of Charlie and that story he told everyone about their trip to London.'

'Now, that's a really funny story, boys,' said Alan, clapping his hands. 'So, what happened to them afterwards, then?'

'Well, they just came home, but this time they caught a train from Paddington to Cardiff, then another train to Aberdare Low Level station and a bus from there back up yere. It took them half the time too. When he spoke to me, he was as angry as a wasp with toothache and for years and years after, for missing that heavyweight fight. Aye! You know, over the years I've had my doubts if they ever went to London in the first place. Who's to say. Perhaps they got off the bus in Cardiff and went on a pub crawl or something.'

CHAPTER 11

The Fox in Cwm Hendre Fawr

THE USUAL GAME of four-handed cribbage was taking place on the large farmhouse table in the main bar of the Plough Inn. The last hand of the night was coming to a close and it appeared that Johnny and Alan were on the losing end of it.

Roy laid his cards on the table, at the same time counting: fifteen two, fifteen four and one for his hat, pointing to the Jack of diamonds in his hand, the same suit as the face card on top of the deck. He grinned at the face Alan pulled as he pegged out, and at Alan showing everyone that he held a dozen points in his hand.

'Bad luck, Al. You can't win 'em all, mind!'

Johnny called across the room. 'Hey, Tref! Put a pint each of whatever these two rascals are drinking over the bar and I'll come over and pay you now, in a minute.' He turned towards the settle nearest to where he was sitting and saw Colin, Jimmy, Titch and George Teale with their heads close together as Jimmy related something he had just heard from his brother-in-law. He'd said that two of his best ewes had been killed by a marauding fox.

'That's a bluddy shame, boys,' said Colin. 'They're all over the damn place since the Forestry planted trees on the mountain.

They can run anywhere in those gutters and you'll never bluddy see 'em.'

'Aye, you're right enough, Colin. Will Mawr told me he saw it running away down his bottom field towards Cwm Hendre Fawr. I'm thinking it could have a den under that big old rock, this side of that small waterfall. Anyway, Will Mawr was asking if I could get a few of us boys to 'ave a look around. He said it's a pretty big fox – he thought it could be that big dog fox we've been chasing since last year. Remember, Col? It could be the one we lost up in the rocks on Craig y Llyn!'

'Aye, aye! I remember that one! Okay, when do you want to go and take a look, then? I'm game for any time you boys want to go. What about you, George?'

'I'm not sure, boys. I'll have to look when I get home what time I have to be in work tomorrow,' he shrugged.

'Well, that's okay, George,' Jimmy replied. 'Three of us with guns and dogs should be enough. Boys, it's Friday night now so what if we went down there first thing in the morning?'

Tyrone, from his spot at the end of the bar, watched them with their heads close together and wondered what was going on. He moved closer to them but they were speaking so quietly he had to ask what they were up to.

Jimmy looked up with a grin. 'If you want to know, Ty, we're getting together in the morning, first thing, to go after a big fox that 'ave killed a couple of ewes. Are you in?'

'Well, yes! Just tell me the time and place to meet you. I don't 'ave a terrier any more, mind – he got run over last week – but I'll have my 12-bore and a pocket full of cartridges.'

'Good enough, Ty!'

'How about seven o'clock by the gate into Cwm Hendre Fawr?'

'Which gate is that, boys?' Tyrone asked.

'It's the one just below Maesyffynon House. Right then, we're all set for the morning.'

Jimmy, his brother Titch, Colin and Tyrone finished their beer and prepared to leave the bar. George stood up and wished them all well for the following day's hunt. 'I might catch up with you tomorrow, okay?'

'Aye, okay, George. See you then.'

Just after 7 a.m. the intrepid hunters began the trek down Cwm Hendre Fawr with their eyes peeled for any sign of the killer fox. Then, as they walked in silence past the waterfall, the dogs began criss-crossing the makeshift dirt road in front of them. Colin, in the lead, held up a hand and they all came to a halt.

'I can smell that bluddy fox,' he whispered. 'He must 'ave just crossed by yere cos it is so strong.'

Suddenly, the fox rose from the grass verge just ahead of them and bolted like greased lightning up the rocky scree towards the rock formation above them. All four dogs took off at high speed after it, yelping with every step. Colin's Rose, being a bit bigger than the other terriers, appeared to be gaining with every stride in the race to catch the fox before he got to his den. Then everything went quiet.

As one, they started scrambling up the scree after the dogs and arrived breathless at the front of the huge rock.

Colin, the first one there, looked around for his two terriers but could only see his tiny Jack Russell. She was marking the entrance under the edge of the rock face and Jimmy's dogs were with her. 'Hey, boys! Did anyone see where Rose went to?'

'No,' said Jimmy. 'We were a bit further down than you and couldn't see the dogs from there.' He bent down to look under the flat slab above the entrance and said, 'Hey, Colin, I'll bet anything that she bolted right in there after that bluddy fox. Yes, that must be where she is!'

Colin nodded his agreement while trying to get his breath back. He knelt down and picked up the little Jack Russell and peered into the blackness under the rock. He then took in a deep breath and called, 'Rose!' He listened for any sound but there was none. He called her name again and thought he heard a faint whimper. Shaking his head, he got to his feet and took off his cap to wipe the sweat from his brow before it dripped in his eyes. He turned and said quietly to the others, 'I think she might have got herself stuck in there somewhere. I'm thinking now she's a bit big in the shoulders to get too far in there. Now we'll have a potch on our hands to get her to come back out.'

Tyrone slowly climbed the scree below them and stood alongside Titch. 'What's happened?' he asked quietly.

'We think one of Colin's dogs has got itself stuck in there,' he replied, pointing to the rock face.

'Well, there's too many of us by yere, so I'll go over there by that big tree and keep a lookout.'

He moved away about 20 feet or so. Jimmy and Titch laid their guns on the grass and grabbed the other dogs.

Colin, still holding the little terrier in his arms, called out Rose's name again. There was still no sound. 'Hey, Jimmy! Come and listen with me a minute!'

He whistled as loud as he could into the darkness beneath the overhang as Jimmy knelt beside him. Jimmy waited a few moments then shook his head. 'Can't yere a bluddy thing, Col! Let's give it a few minutes and try again, is it?'

Ten minutes passed with nothing happening.

'Okay, boys! I'm going back to Hendre Fawr Farm to see if I can borrow some tools. It looks like we'll 'ave to spend some time to dig the little sod out of there,' said Colin.

A full hour passed while Jimmy, Titch and Tyrone, speaking quietly, kept their eyes open for any movement in the surrounding trees and bushes.

Tyrone bent down and looked more closely at a solitary bluebell at his feet, remarking what a lovely flower it was.

Jimmy and Titch looked at each other, grinning like a pair of Cheshire Cats.

'Are you going a bit soft in the head, Tyrone?' said Titch, with a chuckle behind his hand.

Tyrone grinned. 'What? Don't you like beautiful things, Titch?'

'Aye, I do, but there is a time and place for everything, mind.'

Another ten minutes passed before Colin came into view carrying an assortment of implements. He had two shovels, a spade, a mandrel and a wide-bladed *caib* all tied in a bundle across his shoulders. Jimmy stood up and called down to him, 'You took your bluddy time, didn't you? It's been more than an hour since you left yere.'

Colin looked up, grinning, and said, 'Not my fault, boys! 'Ave you ever got out of Hendre Fawr without havin' a cup of tea and tellin' the old lady what you've been doin' lately?'

'S'pose not, Col. There's been no sound at all from under there,' Jimmy replied, gesturing with his thumb over his shoulder. 'So, it looks like we're going to dig our way in and get some of those big stones out of the way to get 'er out, innit?'

Colin nodded agreement as he clambered unsteadily up the loose scree with his burden of tools. Out of breath, he dropped the bundle of tools on the ground and rested, hands on his knees. A minute passed before he reached forward to untie them.

Titch stepped forward, an open-bladed knife in his hand. 'This will be much quicker, Col,' he said, as he cut though the hay-bale twine in one swipe.

BANG! The three of them looked up, startled, to where Tyrone had been leaning casually against the large tree to their left, his twelve-bore held loosely in one hand.

Grinning broadly, he pointed to the narrow ledge above the large rock. 'There's the cause of all our problems, boys.' The limp, lifeless body of the large fox was hanging over the edge of the ledge.

83

'Can you believe it? I was just picking my gun up when I spotted 'im sneaking along that ledge. I didn't 'ave time to put the gun to my shoulder so I let 'im 'ave it from the hip on the run, and I bluddy got 'im! What a lucky shot that was, boys.'

Jimmy looked from Tyrone to the dead fox and back again, judging the distance in his mind. 'Aye, Tyrone. That was a good one, mun. Like something out of the Wild West. What shot are you using then?'

'Heavy duty, of course!' He dipped in his pocket to show him a cartridge. 'See, five eights brass, heavy load. Blue casing.'

'I thought too! You'd never have stopped a fox that big with anything less. Bluddy good shot, Ty.'

Colin turned his back on the fox above his head. 'Never mind 'im now, boys. He's not goin' anywhere any more. So, let's 'ave a look if we can get our Rose out from under this rock, is it?' He dropped to his knees and using the pick end of the miner's small mandrel, he prised out some of the loose rocks from the entrance to the fox's den to make more room to move forward.

He called Titch and Jimmy to come closer and whistled again and again, as loud as he could. 'Did you yere anythin', boys?'

'Not a thing, Col,' Jimmy replied.

'Okay! I'll 'ave to try and open this part wider, then.' Colin swung the pick end of the mandrel into the shale slabs and prised them apart bit by bit. Jimmy and Titch lifted the slab and it broke in two and came away easily.

Colin continued to hack away at the entrance, seemingly oblivious to the pieces of rocks and stones which fell across his head and shoulders. After about four hours of continuous digging by Colin, Jimmy and Titch, the entrance was now wide enough to crawl into. It was now getting too dark to see anything in front of them under the rock face so Colin called a halt to the digging. He looked up at the others and puffed out his cheeks, a sure sign that he had had enough for one day.

'Boys,' he said as he climbed to his feet, 'I don't know about you but I've just about 'ad enough. What say we come back yere in the mornin' and 'ave another crack at it then?'

'Okay by me,' Jimmy and Titch said in unison.

'Sorry, boys, but I won't be able to 'elp you tomorrow,' Tyrone chimed in. 'I've got to go to work and it's double-time pay.' He gave a weak smile as he said it. 'Hey, Colin! What do you want to do about that bluddy fox up there? I don't want it and I wouldn't know what to do with it anyway!'

'Well, Tyrone, I'm too tired to think about it now. What about you, Jimmy?'

'Well, I don't mind collecting a few pounds for it from my brother-in-law, if he pays me, that is. Families can be funny when it comes to giving money away, mind,' he said laughing. 'What we will need in the morning is a decent torch, isn't it?'

Colin, brushing himself down, looked up. 'Aye, you're right enough there. I know, I'll go over to the Pandy on the early colliers' bus from Shop John in the mornin' and see if I can borrow my lamp from the lamp room. I'm pretty sure Old Mock will let me 'ave it for a few hours!'

When Jimmy and Titch arrived at the site the following morning, Colin was already there and all they could see of him were the soles of his working boots, deep into the extended tunnel. Jimmy leaned over and shouted, 'Are you all right in there, Colin?'

His prompt reply was muffled but Jimmy understood enough to know he wanted to be pulled out. He knelt down and grabbed Colin by his ankles and pulled back as hard as he could, with his brother joining in by grabbing one ankle and bracing himself against the rock face. They heard a loud yelp as Colin emerged from the tunnel covered with dirt and bits of shale, with his terrier Rose struggling in his arms as she fought to lick his dust-covered features. He was grinning from ear to ear as he held his face away from her, with the terrier fighting to lick every open area of skin within her reach.

'Well done, Colin!' Jimmy clapped him on his shoulder in delight. 'But coming down yere on your own was a bit *twp*. What if a stone had come down to suffocate you in there?'

'Aye, you're right, but it didn't – and look how pleased she is to see me, boys!'

The little terrier, weak as she was from more than 24 hours underground, was doing her best to climb into his lap as he sat on the tip of debris they had accumulated. Gently he pushed her away and wearily climbed to his feet, at the same time brushing the dirt and stones off his clothes. He looked at the other two men, grinning broadly. 'Der, boys! I could sink a pint of Trefor's best bitter right now and I could guarantee it wouldn't even touch the sides going down.' He took off his cap and wiped the sweat off his face.

Jimmy looked at his watch. 'Well, Col, you'll have to wait another few hours for that bit of pleasure. I think we should all go back home now for a spot of breakfast. What say you, boys?'

'I think that's a good idea, *brawd*,' said Titch, 'a bluddy good idea. My little belly thinks my throat 'ave been cut.'

Carefully they began to climb down the slope, but Rose suddenly sat down and wouldn't even move when Colin called her. Wearily, he climbed back up the scree slope to where she sat, and looked down at the little dog. Her stump of a tail wagged but she made no move at all to follow him. He sighed and bent down to pick her up. 'What do you think of this then, boys? Do me a favour. Can you gather up these tools to take back to Hendre Fawr Farm?'

'Aye, aye. We can do that, Colin,' they said at the same time.

'Better still,' said Titch, 'if we tell them all about this little escapade, we'll end up having a nice cup of tea from the old lady. She just loves to hear all the *clecs* about something local.'

Chapter 12

Blucher's terriers

LATER THAT SUNDAY night in the main bar of the Plough Inn, Colin was just finishing the pint of best bitter he had so craved earlier in the day when in came Jimmy, Johnny and Alan. Jimmy pointed a finger at Colin and asked him if the pint had tasted as good as he thought it would that morning.

'Better, Jimmy. Much, much better,' he replied, smacking his lips with satisfaction as he made his way to the bar for a refill.

'A pint of best, if you please, Mr Williams.'

'There's polite, Mr Howells,' said Trefor. 'Must be because it's a Sunday, right, boys?'

'Right enough, Mr Williams,' Johnny replied laughing. 'It should be like this every day, don't you think? A pint for Alan, Jimmy and myself, if you please.'

Sipping their beer, they all moved slowly across the room to sit around the big table and watch the usual game of cribbage in progress.

Johnny turned to Colin. 'I yerd from a little bird something about your Sunday morning escapades in down in Cwm Hendre Fawr, Col!'

Colin looked around Johnny's wide shoulder at Jimmy and whispered loudly, 'Bluddy cleckerbox!'

Jimmy, not taking any offence, grinned back at him and said, 'Well, it was *clecs* worth telling, wasn't it? Somehow, between us, we managed to rescue that little bitch of yours from under those rocks. She's the one with the papers, isn't it?'

'Aye, it is, and I don't need reminding, thank you very much! But while we're on the subject, thanks to you and Titch for all your help. I couldn't have done it without you two, so thanks from me and thanks from Rose, too.'

Everybody around the table broke up laughing at that reference to his terrier.

Trefor, pulling a fresh pint for Willi Bray, called out. 'Hey, Colin! I saw a report in the *Aberdare Leader* this week about you again. You're most certainly putting this little village in the spotlight! One and eleven pence, please, Willi.' He reached out and swept the small pile of coins into the open till drawer without making any attempt to count them.

Alan leaned forward to look directly at Colin, nodding his head towards the landlord. 'What's he on about then, Colin?'

Colin laughed and pulled his cap down tighter over his eyes. 'I dunno. Mind, I did speak to a couple of the *Leader's* reporters, but that was weeks ago. Could be something that I knew about or did ages ago.' He raised his voice. 'What was it about, Tref?'

'Can't remember. I'll find it after. I'm a bit busy at the moment. You boys are drinking too fast, so I have to put a new barrel on. Wait a minute, okay?' He lifted the trapdoor in the floor behind the bar and disappeared from sight down the wooden stairs into the darkness, a heavy torch in his hand.

Johnny nudged Alan. 'That's not a very safe way to go down there, is it?'

'Probably not,' Alan replied. 'But at least it keeps him fit. It's not as if he has to do that every five minutes, is it?'

Trefor reappeared like a jack-in-the-box, smiling broadly. 'Right then. Who's next?'

'Only me, Trefor!' Old John Shinkins was leaning with both hands on the bar, but only his cap and shoulders could be seen.

Trefor, a concerned look on his features, asked, 'What's wrong, John? Are you ill or something?'

'Oh, it's nothing to worry about, Trefor. I've got a bit of a bad back, that's all.'

Trefor gave him his drink then reached under the bar for the *Leader*. 'Yere you are, Colin: "Hunting foxes on Craig y Llyn is not a game, says Mr Howells from the Bryn, Rhyd-y-groes."'

'Don't say any more, Tref. I know what that's about now. The Howells they're writin' about in that paper is my father, Fred. Some chap on the *Leader* says he wants to do a story on the number of foxes that 'ave been killed, shot or trapped around yere in the past five years. Some bluddy 'opes, I say. I told 'im I didn't 'ave any idea how many Fred 'ad got or how many Jimmy and Titch 'ad got between them, or how many I 'ad shot over the years. In the end, I told 'im to go and ask the local farmers or better still go and ask the Fox Destruction Society how many tails they 'ad paid out on.' He laughed. 'But that might not do 'im any good either, cos that club covers all the areas from Penderyn to Cwmdare and across Merthyr mountain as well as Rhyd-y-groes and Craig y Llyn and this parish. Der, everyone knows that my father killed loads of foxes, not only on this mountain...' he nodded his head sideways in the direction where he thought the Llyn was, '...but all the way to Cwmdare and above the Rhondda Valley.'

Johnny put his glass back on the table. 'Tell me, Col, do these reporters pay you well for all of these stories or interviews you give them?'

'Pay me? You must be bluddy jokin', Johnny. Fat chance of that 'appening. And yere's another thing! You tell 'em a story and it always comes out in print different to what you told them. So why bluddy ask in the first place, innit? Now if my father was alive, he could tell a few stories that might sound a bit far-fetched but were all true enough.'

'Like what then, Colin?' Alan asked, tongue in cheek, while winking at the others as he egged Colin on to relate a story.

Colin looked closely at him then grinned. 'Okay then, what about this one. I'm willin' to bet any amount that no one yere 'as yerd this story about Fred. He was 'aving a pint in the Prince of Wales in Waun-gron – this was a long time ago, mind. Some chap he was sittin' by was talkin' about Blucher. Remember 'im, boys?'

'I remember him, Colin!' Old John Shinkins chipped in. 'Remember, I'm from Waun-gron! What a character, in his 50-year-old military coat and his knee-high boots. And how many foxes did he shoot in 'is lifetime? Hundreds and hundreds, I dare say! He was a great friend of your dad's, isn't it, Col?'

'Aye, he was,' said Colin, touching his cap in John's direction. 'Well, anyway, this chap said he'd yerd that Blucher 'ad died, like, the week before. It seems he 'adn't been well for some time and 'ad gone over to stay at his sister's place in Defynnog...'

'Defynnog? Where's that, Col?' Alan cut in.

Colin paused in his tale, wondering if Alan was serious in his questioning. 'It's over towards Brecon, Alan, and to get there you 'ave to turn off at Libanus on the way down the seven-mile pitch into Brecon Town. Anyway, this chap told Fred he was pretty certain that Blucher 'ad indeed died, and went on to say he 'ad a distant relative livin' somewhere down in the Maescynon area, but he didn't know their name. Fred told 'im, "Don't bother mate. I'll find out who it is."'

'Well, he went to a few 'ouses but they 'ad no idea who Fred was talkin' about. So, he asked at the next 'ouse who was the oldest person they knew still livin' on the council estate. It took 'im ages and by then it was dark, so he went 'ome. The next day he went back down there. He 'ad to walk everywhere cos he was skint…'

'As usual,' Alan murmured.

Colin looked at Alan around Johnny's shoulder. 'As I was sayin'... he went back down to Maescynon to look for that relative of old Blucher. He said he asked at nearly every 'ouse in one area until somebody told 'im who the oldest person around there was. It was Jimmy Smith...'

'I know 'im too!' Old John Shinkins slapped his knee in triumph. 'Him and me worked together in the old Tower Colliery and then I moved yere to Rhyd-y-groes and got a job in the Pandy...'

'Aye, all right, John. Can I finish my story now?'

'Well, aye. Don't let me stop you, mun.'

'Right, then,' Colin grinned with good humour. 'Well, Fred found out where Jimmy Smith lived and went to 'ave a chat with 'im. Jimmy told Fred where this distant relative of Blucher's lived – it was a bit further towards Merthyr. They 'ad a small farm and kept loads of chickens and sold eggs and little chicks for a living but Jimmy Smith didn't know their name. Fred told me he knocked on their door and an old lady only opened it a crack to look at 'im, so he stood on the front step and asked them about Blucher. She told 'im Blucher 'ad died the week before and closed the door in his face! Fred told me that he just stood there on the step for a bit but he never saw that old woman again. So after he got 'ome, he decided to go over to Defynnog to see Blucher's sister and ask her if he could 'ave his terriers to look after. He said he'd buy them if he 'ad to.'

'How could he do that if he was skint, then? I think that was a bit of a cheek to ask for his dogs, wasn't it?' Jimmy said, softening his question with a broad grin.' After all, they were the best terriers around yere, weren't they?'

'Aye, I suppose you're right there, Jimmy. But in Fred's mind, he was the best bloke around yere to take good care of them. At least, that's what he told me. He 'ad known Blucher since he was a young man...'

'And I still think it was a bluddy cheek to go there, especially since the poor man had only just died – but do go on with your story, Col.'

'So Fred set out really early the next day to walk across the Brecon Beacons to Defynnog. I think he said that from our 'ouse on the Bryn in Rhyd-y-groes to Defynnog it must be more than 25 miles.'

'And he walked all that way?' said Alan.

'Oh, aye. He said he tried to thumb a lift but they all drove right past him. He said that when he got to Defynnog he asked a few people where Blucher's sister lived. At first nobody could tell 'im anything until he explained who she was and that was when they realised he was talking about *yr hen wrach*…'

'What the heck is that, then?' Alan asked.

'It means "the old witch", Old John Shinkins said, before anyone else could explain. 'You've got to be a Welsh speaker to know that, Alan. You've yerd of Cwmgwrach haven't you? Well, that means "valley of the witch". Go on, Colin.'

'Well, in the end he found her 'ouse, if you can call it that. Apparently it was a bit of a hovel outside the village and when she came to the door, he could see why they called her the old witch. He said he could 'ardly see her face because she 'ad a yuge mop of grey hair that 'ung all over the place and that she looked as if she 'adn't 'ad a good scrub in ages. He said she shuffled along and she was bent over to 'alf her height. He said he told her who he was and that he knew her brother from years back when they went together on 'unting trips. Then he asked her if he could have her brother's terriers to look after. With that, she swung her walkin' stick at his 'ead and told 'im to get away from her door!

'Next thing, he offered to buy the two dogs from her and 'ad to duck pretty quick when she swung her stick at his 'ead again, and he stepped back pretty sharpish out of range.

'He said he tried again to tell her he'd 'unted all sorts of game with her brother for years and both dogs knew him well enough. But she was 'aving none of it and told 'im to go away, cos he wouldn't be 'aving the dogs. So, in the end he gave up and walked all the way back 'ome with nothin' to show after all those miles across the mountains.'

'I don't suppose he was all that pleased, then,' said Alan, laughing at the image in his mind of Fred ducking sharpish under a swinging walking stick.

'Not one bit!' Colin grinned. 'But, fair play, he 'ad to try and get 'em cos they were the best terriers around yere at that time. It did affect 'im for a few weeks, mind, because he kept on about 'em whenever he 'ad a few pints under his belt. Der, he said she was the worst-looking woman he 'ad ever seen and he 'ad seen his share, believe me. He said he wasn't afraid of her like some of the villagers in Defynnog, but he was willing to bet the local kids kept well away from her 'ouse. Aye, indeed. When he first described her to me it sent a shiver through me and I never saw the woman – or her brother Blucher, for that matter. Fred told me he had eyes like an animal.'

'Old Fred was right enough there, boys!' Old John Shinkins remarked, nodding his head. 'I remember him about the place in Waun-gron. He never seemed to bother with anyone, except Fred and a couple of other fox and rabbit hunters and of course the local Squire, who had a pack of hounds he could call on for a bit of hunting now and then.' Old John started coughing and began thumping his chest with the side of his fist. 'This bluddy dust in my lungs is just killing me at times, boys.'

Colin nodded in sympathy, having worked for years underground in the same area. 'Aye, it will get us all in the end, John.'

CHAPTER 13

Desert Flower

M ONDAY NIGHT IN the Plough Inn was practice night for the team that played in the Waun-gron Darts League. Given that they'd had a number of dismal years in that particular league, the team decided, after some lengthy and heated meetings, that it might be best if they concentrated on a nucleus of six players and just one substitute, when his shiftwork schedule would allow him the time to play. The transformation in the team was nothing short of miraculous. They went from losing most of their league games to winning nearly everything in sight. After winning the first three games and not losing a single leg in the process, this proved to all the naysayers in the club that this was the way to go if they wanted to win any trophies. To this end, it was decided to keep the same team order for every future game. In Twm, they had the perfect first man, who could hit a double with his first dart almost every time. He was followed by three very high-scoring players and the final two men in the team could be depended on, most of the time, to go out with three darts or less.

This particular Monday night was no exception. The usual group of players took turns to throw darts at their favourite areas of the corkboard's doubles or the high-scoring (and very small) treble-twenty space.

At the other end of the long room, the usual game of four-handed cribbage was taking place on the big farmhouse table. At that moment Dai Chops was loudly proclaiming the ability of his friend's racing greyhound, who, he said, 'would beat anything on four legs' at the racetrack in Skewen on the coming Friday night.

'Well, boys! This dog is an absolute winner and I'm going down there to put a few quid on him to win, no matter what the bluddy odds are. What about that, then? Who else is in with me to win some money then? It's a real certainty, boys.'

Johnny laughed. 'There's no such thing as a certainty, Dai, except dying, and that's a long way off. Well, it is for me, anyway!'

'How can you be so sure, Dai?' Alan looked up at him from his seat at the card table.

'Cos we have a secret plan, that's why.'

'Come off it, Dai!' Alan scoffed. 'What bluddy secret? Let us in on that and I for one will be willing to lose a few quid myself. If it sounds at all feasible, that is!' Alan smiled and returned to his card game without another word.

'Fifteen two for that, Col.'

'Thank you,' Colin said, as he moved one of the scoring pegs two spaces.

'All right! All right!' Dai Chops whispered, behind his hand, 'Here's the bluddy secret, if you must know. I make my way to a spot just past the winning post and when the dogs come out of the traps, I whistle as loud as I can manage and my mate's dog will run like 'ell to come to me. This dog is quick enough to beat all of them but my whistling will just make sure he wins. After that we go to the bookies to pick up our winnings! How does that sound? Easy as pie, innit?'

'Some bluddy 'opes,' said Colin, from the other side of the big table.

'No no! It's right enough! I'm telling you, this dog is a bluddy winner every time he races on this track – honest to God, boys. I wouldn't be bragging about it or putting good money on him if it wasn't true.'

'So how much money are *you* putting at risk, Dai?' Johnny turned in his seat to look directly at him.

Dai Chops hesitated, then said, 'If I've still got it on Friday, I'm gonna put a fiver on him.'

'A fiver? That's almost a week's pay for some people, innit?'

Dai Chops laughed out loud. 'Aye, aye. It is for some people. It all depends where you're working, boys.'

'All right, I'm in for a couple of quid. What about you, Al?' Johnny winked across the table at his brother-in-law.

'Aye, okay then. I'm in for a couple of quid too.'

Dai looked around the bar as he raised his voice. 'Who else is in, then?'

Colin looked up from the game. 'Okay then, I'm in for a pound, Dai. So, what's the name of this bluddy wonder dog?'

'Well, I call 'im Lightning...'

'Lightnin'? Can you imagine it, boys? Dai by yere down at the local park, calling out, "Yere, boy! C'mon, Lightnin'!" Everybody who yerd that would be laughing their bluddy socks off. Okay then, Dai, what's his racin' name? He 'as got a racin' name, 'aven't he?' Bobby put his cards down on the table to hold his sides in laughter.

By this time Dai Chops was looking totally embarrassed by the questioning. 'Of course he has,' he said defensively. 'His racing name is...' he paused, then muttered, '... his racing name is Desert Flower.'

The crowd around the table and the others in the bar erupted with laughter. Alan, laying his cards down, began to wipe the tears of mirth which streamed freely down his cheeks as he repeated, 'Desert Flower! This is a dog is it, not a bitch?'

'Of course it is!' Dai looked at the crowd of grinning faces around him and repeated indignantly, 'Of course it is, boys!'

Alan started laughing again as he said, 'Sorry, Dai. I can't help it but I had to ask. So, there's nothing queer about him, then?'

'Hey! C'mon boys,' Dai was desperately trying to get some sort of seriousness back into their conversation, but wasn't having much luck in that direction.

'Boys, he's a genuine racing greyhound and my money will be on him to win on Friday night. So, who wants to win a few quid with me?'

'Okay, okay, joking aside, Dai. We've already told you, mun. Alan and me are in for a few quid but I'm thinking we can't all put our money on in the same place, can we? That would only shorten the odds, wouldn't it?'

'Aye, it would. I know I would want to lay it off pretty sharpish if I was taking a rush of betting on the same horse.' Alan from time to time would run a private 'book', especially on the major horse races, out of his own pocket. It was all a bit dubious because he didn't have a licence to operate as a bookie. He just did it for the thrill of the bet, in the same way as two friends would bet against each other on the outcome of two local rugby teams – he just expanded the number of bets he felt he could handle.

'Okay, boys!' Alan raised his voice. 'Here's the plan for Friday. You, Dai! I want you to find out by Wednesday, if you can, what the odds are on…' he paused to prevent himself laughing out loud, '… Desert Flower! We need this information so that we can place our bets, small as they are, with a few different bookies, right? For instance, we can use the off-track betting shop in Waun-gron. For those who don't know, it's next door to the Globe Inn. I know of one in Neath by the market and there's another one in Glynneath by the fish and chip shop. We can also use the bookies at the racetrack in Skewen, so there is no shortage of places where we can put a bet on, is there? So, who's willing to have a bet on this wonder dog, then?' More than half a dozen hands shot up in an instant.

Johnny laughed. 'Boys, you would swear we are organising a multi-million pound scheme, when we'll be lucky if a total of twenty quid will be at risk on Dai's say so.'

'Okay, boys,' said Alan. 'Just gimme a minute and I'll make a list. Mr Williams! Do you have a writing pad I could take a page out of, please? Or any old scrap of plain paper will do.'

Trefor nodded, reaching under the bar and producing a pen and a lined writing pad, like some magician pulling a rabbit out of a top hat.

'Right, then! Let's see who we've got so far. Dai Chops, Johnny, Colin, myself, Bobby, Twm, Roy? Are you in?'

'Yes. Put me down for a couple of quid. I'll give it to you now in a minute when I get some change from Trefor. Okay?'

'No problem. Okay, who else is there? C'mon boys. This is a no-brainer. Right, Willi, you're in for a pound and Danny and Elwyn and Dai-vid all for a pound each… How the 'ell did you get that nickname, Dai?'

'Too many David Thomases about at the same time. I was called Dai-vid so there's no mistake, I suppose. So, Alan, put me in for three pounds, then. Cos I can't let you boys have all the fun bragging about how much you won on this wonder dog, can I?'

'What about your missus, then? If she finds out you're betting on a dog race with her money?' Twm, grinning like the Cheshire Cat, turned to face him.

Dai shrugged and took out his wallet and gave Alan three crisp pound notes. 'Lay this on for me, Alan, just in case I'll be stuck in work.'

'Okay, Dai-vid.' Alan stuffed the notes in his back pocket. 'So, here's the plan. We'll find out the odds – but it doesn't matter really what they are. Dai Chops will do that later this week, on

Wednesday. After that, I will do my best to lay our bets on in as many different places I can find. Then on Friday... What time is this wonder dog racing, Dai?'

'I think he's in the fourth race.'

'Aye, aye, but what time is that, mun?'

'Oh. About 7.30 to 8 o'clock, I suppose.'

'Okay, then. Good enough. Listen, all those who want to go to Skewen, we'll meet yere early on Friday night, have a pint and take two cars to the track. Is everybody clear on that? Are there any questions? None? Well, that's good, then. Okay, boys, whose deal is it?' Alan asked, shuffling the deck of cards.

Friday evening arrived and there was an air of excitement in the Plough Inn as they prepared to leave the bar for Skewen. They piled into Alan and Johnny's cars to make their way down the valley towards the market town of Neath. Dai Chops, in Alan's car, asked him how much money he thought was going on Desert Flower.

'I'm not exactly sure, Dai, but our little group is betting sixteen quid on him as the 13/2 second favourite. So there must be quite a bit of money going on him. In my experience the bookies are pretty sharp on setting the odds.'

'Damn! That's almost two week's pay for some people, so we will do all right when he wins.'

'Well, you have told us enough that he's certain to win. Let's hope it turns out like you said.'

Dai pulled a face. 'He's a bluddy great dog, Alan.'

Minutes later they found parking for the cars and joined the crowd entering the racetrack. They all made their way down to the rails to watch one of the early races. Several of them having never been to a dog track before, they wanted to get a sense of the excitement as the dogs were released from the traps to chase the electric hare.

Alan looked at his watch and said, 'I think we're yere a little bit early boys. Let's get away from this spot, is it?' He turned away, with Johnny and Dai Chops following him as he made his way up the spectators' embankment. The three of them looked towards the starting area. In the distance they could see the handlers parading the dogs for the next race in the small area behind the main stand.

Dai Chops grabbed Alan's arm and pointed in their direction. 'Hey, boys!' he said excitedly. 'Look, there's our bluddy winner! He's the biggest one!'

'They all look the same size to me,' Alan said, shielding his eyes from the floodlights on the grandstand.

'Is he the dark brown one that's making all the fuss?' Johnny pointed to one dog that was doing his best to get away from his handler's grip.

'No, no. Ours is the big black one. He's got a white blaze on his chest.'

'Got it!' Johnny said. 'You're right, Dai – he's a lot bigger than the rest of them.'

Dai grinned. 'Well, I don't think there's any law against that, is there?' He looked again to where the handlers were getting the dogs ready. 'Hey boys, I'd better get moving to get my place on the finish line, innit!' He turned and almost ran down the sloped embankment.

Johnny watched him until he disappeared into the crowd and then murmured, 'Well, Alan, I hope this is not a wasted journey down yere.'

'Me too,' his brother-in-law replied. 'C'mon, let's go down a bit further. Those lights are a bit too bright up yere.'

Finally, the moment had arrived and the dogs, after being paraded for everyone to see, were loaded into the traps. The bell rang shrilly, the gates opened and out sprang the line of dogs. It took only a second and the big black dog was already a length in front of the others. He continued to stride away from the pack when suddenly above the clamour of the crowd they heard a shrill piercing whistle. Desert Flower surged ahead by at least three or four yards until he was about 10 yards from the finish line – when he suddenly changed direction and jumped over the barricade into the open arms of Dai Chops, knocking him flat on his back on the ground and licking his face all over.

The crowd standing nearby erupted, with everyone shouting about it being a false race. Some were yelling they wanted their money back from the bookies, who were standing with their mouths open at the spectacle of Dai Chops lying on the ground with the greyhound in his arms.

The betting crowd from the Plough were dumbfounded at this unexpected turn around in their fortunes. What had looked an absolute certainty was now in tatters. Johnny and Alan looked at each other and started laughing as Bobby and the others threw their race cards down in disgust.

Then out of the crowd milling around them came Dai Chops, grinning, with the big black dog still in his arms.

Colin grabbed his arm. 'What the 'ell was that nonsense then, Dai?'

'Well, there was too much of a crowd on the finish line and ten yards was the closest I could get to it. Sorry, boys, but you can see how much he loves me and he's not even my bluddy dog.' He turned his head away as the big hound tried again to lick his face. He looked over his shoulder and said quietly. 'Look out boys, yere comes the owner – looking for his dog, I 'spect. *Shomai*, Dick! Boys, this is Dick Rogers, the owner of this lovely dog.' He put the dog on the ground with his arm around him and offered to shake hands with Dick.

Dick brushed the outstretched hand aside and in an almost angry tone said, 'What the 'ell did you bluddy whistle for, Dai? He was winning the bluddy race by a mile without you doing that! I knew it was you as soon as I yerd it. Damn it all, Dai! I lost a bluddy packet on that race and now the stewards are going to have an inquiry about it too. So you'd better get your story straight if they come looking for you, mate!' He pulled the big greyhound away from Dai's arms. He strapped a wide leather collar on his dog and stalked away without another word to Dai or the small group with him.

Dai lifted his shoulders resignedly. 'I'm really very sorry, boys. It shouldn't have turned out like this…'

'Well, in my opinion,' said Alan, straight-faced. 'I think you should be buying all of us a few pints each when we get back to the Plough tonight. What do you think, boys?'

'Right enough too.' Colin looked at Dai Chops' downcast features and started laughing. 'C'mon, you daft sod. We're kiddin' you!'

When they got back to the Plough they all entered the bar together. 'Hey!' Trefor shouted. 'Yere come the conquering heroes. How much did you win, boys?'

'Not a bluddy thing, Tref,' Colin replied, desperately trying to keep a straight face.

'No! So the dog lost the race! After all Dai Chops' bragging that he was a dead cert!'

'Not exactly, Tref,' Johnny replied. 'He didn't finish the race.'

Trefor looked from one to the other as if trying to divine the meaning behind Johnny's words. 'Okay, boys! Tell me the truth of what happened, then.'

'Remember Dai telling us about his secret trick to get the dog to run faster?'

'Aye, aye! He said he would whistle his mate's dog home.'

'Right enough, Tref. What he didn't say was, he had to be on the finish line or better still on the other side of it when he whistled to it. Unfortunately for us, he was about 10 yards from the finish line when he whistled. What happened next is hilarious: the bluddy dog jumped the rails right into his arms and knocked him flat on his back, and got disqualified by the stewards! Tref, you should have yerd the commotion from the crowd!'

Trefor started laughing so hard he had to hold onto the counter for support. Meanwhile, Dai stood in the middle of the bar looking shamefaced as everyone in the bar pointed an accusing finger at him.

It took Trefor a few minutes to get his breath back and then he said, 'Well, boys, that is the funniest story I have ever yerd in the 20-odd years I have been the landlord of this bluddy pub! Pints all round, is it? My treat, okay boys?'

CHAPTER 14

About Fred

COLIN LAID HIS cards face down on the table and, folding his arms, sat back in his chair. 'In answer to your question, Twm. Yes, my father was always willin' to have a bet on just about anythin'.'

'Well, there you are, then! I can remember Fred comin' yere on one Saturday afternoon with a bluddy yuge rat. He was sittin' on the windowsill outside with the cage by his feet. This yuge rat was alive in the wire cage. Boys, it was this big.' He held his hands in front of him about two feet apart.

Colin laughed out loud. 'Hey, Twm! Wait a bluddy minute! We'll 'ave to put some 'andcuffs on you before long, to stop you exaggeratin' so much.'

'Well, it was a bluddy big rat, is what I'm tryin' to say. Boys, you should have seen Fred. He was full of it! He had his two terriers with him and they were doin' their best to get at that rat in the wire cage. Jimmy by there came out of the bar with his two terriers and they saw the rat too. You should have yerd the row. What with Fred shoutin' the odds and the bluddy dogs all barkin' at the same time, there was a place. Talk about a row! Fred was bettin' two shillings with anyone on which dog would get to that rat first. Then somebody else came out with a pair of dogs. I can't remember who it was now. Hey, Trefor! Remember when

Fred had that bluddy big rat out by yere? Can you remember that other bloke?'

Trefor put the glass he was polishing on the bar and puffed out his cheeks. 'Not a chance, Twm. Could have been Elwyn, he sometimes brings his two dogs with him, or it could've been a chap passing through off the mountain. I don't know for sure, Twm.' He shrugged and turned to serve Old John Shinkins.

'Anyway,' Twm went on, 'that Fred was taking bets like you wouldn't believe! In the end he said, "That's it, boys, no more bets. Right, yere we go. I'm goin' to let this bluddy rat go and give it a head start, right! Let it cross the road before we turn the dogs loose, is it? Then he said to Willi Bray, "Hey, you, Willi. I want you to hold my two terriers while I turn the rat loose, okay? Now then, is everybody ready? Okay, keep a sharp eye on which dog gets to it first."

'Boys, it was like a bluddy circus out there on the road in front of the Plough. Fred was shoutin' the odds, and all the dogs barkin'. It was enough to wake all those lyin' in the cemetery half a mile away, and I'm pretty sure that poor bluddy rat must have been absolutely terrified. Well, Fred opened the cage and the rat skelped it pretty quick across the road and went under Johnny Wills' car with about half a dozen dogs after it. That was when all 'ell broke out about whose dog got to it first. I'm tellin' you, boys, what a bluddy commotion with old Fred arguin' the toss in favour of his tiny Jack Russell terrier – what was her name again, Col?'

Colin smiled. 'That little bitch was forever and a day Fred's favourite dog. Her name was Judy.'

'Aye, aye, that's it! Fred was arguin' that because she was the smallest dog out there, that she got under Johnny's car quicker than any of the others and killed it. So she was first! In the end nobody could agree which dog was first and Fred had to give all the two-shilling bets back.'

Everyone around the table started laughing at the outcome of Twm's tale.

Twm smiled as he looked at the faces of his audience. 'Aye, that Fred was a bluddy character all right. He'd have a bet on anythin' if he thought there was the slightest chance of makin' a few bob.'

'Right, boys! Back to business. Whose lead was it?'

'Mine,' Colin replied, picking up his cards.

Johnny and Alan at the far end of the bar had joined in the laughter as Twm completed his tale.

'You know Trefor, it's amazing after – what is it now? Two years since we buried Fred? – just how many times I've yerd his name mentioned in yere, nearly every week.'

'You're right enough, Johnny.' Trefor nodded his head in Colin's direction. 'He told me only last week that people, some of them he didn't even know, would come up to him to relate some yarn or other about Fred. He was well known all over the place and there was no real harm in him at all, was there? Although, I have to say, some of his antics would make some people pretty annoyed with him.'

'True,' said Johnny. 'I remember one instance. Fred came in one Saturday night and as usual, the bar was packed. He pulled a rabbit out of his pocket and stood on a chair in the middle of the room and called for order. He held up the rabbit for everyone to see and said he was going to raffle it off for a shilling a ticket. He said all the money raised would go to the Rhyd-y-groes Old Age Pensioners fund. Well, he sold the best part of a book of tickets. And he gave me all the money to hold in trust.'

'Oh, aye. I remember that, now you're saying. You gave that money to me to put in that box I always use. Yes, I think he collected about £3 in all.'

Alan laughed. 'I was yere that night and I can remember very well who won the raffle too! Hey, Colin! Do you remember that raffle for a rabbit that Fred organised in yere a few years back? Can you tell me who won it?'

Colin looked up from his card game and said, with a grin on his face, 'I think I did, Alan. Why are you askin' now?'

'Oh, we're just following on from Twm's yarn about your father and his antics over the years. I said he could cause a row without even trying with some of his get-rich-quick schemes.'

'Aye. You're right enough boys. My father could cause a row with the Pope without even tryin'. I often told 'im that it would 'ave been touch and go between 'im and the bloke who started World War II, who could cause the most trouble.'

Everyone in the bar broke up laughing at that one.

Trefor sighed. 'Yes, he was a character all right, and sometimes I really miss his old nonsense in yere. There are not many around like him.'

Johnny and Alan both raised their glasses in silent tribute to the memory of Fred Howells.

CHAPTER 15

About Horses

IT WAS FRIDAY night in the Plough Inn. The usual crowd had gathered around the big farmhouse table and a game of four-handed cribbage was in full swing. The chat around the table was centred on the following day's horse racing at the famous Epsom Downs course, where the annual Derby was to take place. David Samuel Noel Goliath Jones, known locally as Dai Bandit, sitting at the far end of the table, took a swig of his beer and asked, 'Does anyone know the history of the Derby?'

'I doubt it,' Johnny replied, 'but I'm sure that you're about to enlighten us with your greater sports knowledge.'

'Well, this event is the original Derby. The inaugural race was held in 1780 and was named after Lord Derby. Today there are many events around the world which use the name Derby – that includes all other sports too.' He gave them a toothless grin and added, 'Boys, this information is by courtesy of Her Majesty the Queen's library in Swansea nick.'

Colin, his cap pulled down tight over his eyes, looked up and said 'My father knew a lot about 'orses too.'

'Get away from yere, Colin!' Roy snorted derisively. 'Fred, if I remember correctly, lost far more bets than he ever won. I remember telling him once that he couldn't pick his nose tidy. Bless his soul. Wherever he is,' he added, looking up at the ceiling.

'No, no, I know that! What I'm talkin' about is not about bettin', mun. When he was workin' in the Tower Colliery – that was years and years ago, mind – he got pretty friendly with old Tom Williams, who was the 'ostler at the Tower stables. He's gone now too, poor dab. Anyway, Fred told me, no end of times, mind, that he could remember the name of every 'orse in the stable and the ones workin' underground too.' He grinned impishly. 'I don't know what you're going to do with that useless piece of information, Roy, but my father thought he was pretty clever to remember the names of forty 'orses. He was proud to 'ave a memory like that.'

Trefor, listening from behind the bar called out. 'Aye, Colin! If he had that good a memory, I have to wonder why he didn't remember to settle up with me when he got his pay?'

Everyone in the bar broke into laughter at Trefor's remark.

'Hey, boys, that's not fair!' Colin said in defence of his father. 'He 'ad a 'ell of a job with what little pay he 'ad from his lousy job underground. That's why he took on that extra security job with the NCB, to 'elp out with a bit of extra cash.'

'Hey, boys!' Bobby, Colin's playing partner, raised his voice to change the subject. 'Who's got a good tip for tomorrow's Derby?'

'No idea yet, Bobby,' Roy replied, playing a card. 'Fifteen two. Peg two for that, if you please, Twm. I'll tell you tomorrow afternoon when I've had a good look at my *Racing Gazette*.'

Old John Shinkins leaned forward from his seat on the wooden settle alongside the stove. 'I've got one, boys!'

Roy turned sideways to look at him. 'Okay, John. What horse have you got, then?'

'Sea Bird! Sea Bird, that's my pick, boys, for tomorrow.'

Dai Bandit laughed. 'I don't know how old your paper is, John. Sea Bird won last year's Derby and I haven't yerd that nag even mentioned for this year's field of runners.'

'Well, there you are, then. Shows how much I know, innit?'

'Aye, leave it there, John! My little daughter Susie could probably pick more winners than you!'

'When I was talkin' about all those 'orses up at the Tower Colliery, I meant to tell you this little story about my father,' interjected Colin. 'Me and Fred were walkin' down Cwm Hendre Fawr and Fred decided to cut across Twm Rees' field. Well, Twm 'ad a pretty big Welsh cob in that field and I knew full well that she didn't like anyone or anythin' to be in there with her. Except Twm Rees, that is. Well, I got across there pretty sharpish cos I could see her picking up her 'ead and lookin' towards us. Fred, as usual, was dawdlin' along, stoppin' to look at this and that. I saw Twm's mare turnin' towards us and I shouted for 'im to bluddy move it. Of course, 'im bein' Fred, he took no notice.

'That was, until he yerd her gallopin' like 'ell towards 'im. He was about 10 or 15 yards from the gate when he looked over his shoulder. She was bearin' down on him, her neck outstretched and her yers flat to her 'ead. Boys, I 'ave never seen anyone move so fast in wellies in my life. He took off like an Olympic sprinter in the mud and was over that gate in a flash. One 'and on the top rail and he sailed over it to land in a heap in a puddle on the other side. Then – the cheeky sod – when he got up, he started shoutin' at me for not saying somethin' about the bluddy 'orse comin' after 'im. She'd 'ave 'ad 'im too. She was a bluddy big 'orse, mind.'

Everyone, knowing Fred, began laughing at the very thought of seeing Fred flying through the air in his wellies.

At the far end of the bar, Johnny turned to face his brother-in-law. 'I don't think I've ever told anyone about my little experience with a horse.'

Trefor moved closer, still drying a pint glass. 'Well, go on Johnny,' he said, smiling. 'This should be good.'

'Well, years and years ago, long before I ever began to think of getting married...'

'That *was* long ago,' Alan interrupted with a smile.

'Haisht a minute, Alan! Let him finish, mun!'

'Anyway, two new girls arrived in the village and moved into that farm out on the *waun* in the middle of the village. I can't remember the name of it now – something Uchaf – but you know the one, Tref.'

Trefor nodded.

'On this particular Saturday night on the way home from the dance in Glynneath, I got to chatting with one of them on the bus on the way home and asked her if I could walk her home. It was about eleven o'clock at night, and pitch black as we went down Cwm Isaac and across the field and past the other farm over the bridge and that small river down there. She knew exactly where the path to her farm was and I followed close behind her. Well, we got to the farm okay and I turned to go back...'

'No kiss goodnight, then?' Alan winked at Trefor.

Johnny pulled a face. 'Well, you know how it is, boys! Anyway, on the way back I followed the path in the dark for a while, using the street light by the chapel as a guide for direction. Then somehow, I got off the path and in the dark, I went almost tiptoe down this shallow slope and then stopped to listen. I could hear some water running and I thought I knew exactly where I was.

'Hearing the sound of this little brook I thought I would only have to go up the bank the other side and I would be able to see Teddy Newth's farm. So, I took a couple of steps back and ran to jump blindly over the brook. Unfortunately for me, when I landed on the other side, I'd jumped right into the side of a bluddy horse that was standing there. I jumped back over the brook in a hurry and the horse galloped off into the night.'

Everyone listening to the tale began roaring with laughter, much to Johnny's chagrin.

Trefor holding his sides said weakly. 'Well, go on! What happened next?'

'Oh, it took me ages to find my way back to Cwm Isaac and up the hill to our house. My father was still up and looked down at my shoes and trousers, which were covered in mud and cowshit. He didn't say a word, mind, but I'll bet you anything he was just dying to ask me where I'd been.'

Alan clapped him on the shoulder. 'Let that be a lesson to you not to take strange girls home.'

'Aye, you've got that right, Al.'

Trefor leaned forward, still polishing a glass, and said in a loud whisper. 'I think betting good money on horse racing is a mug's game! Wasn't there a bookmaker somewhere who named his house Mug's Hall?'

'I think you're quite right, Trefor. A long time ago I was taking bets, but only from friends and some people that I knew quite well. I used to pay out only on the odds that were in the papers. It was all unofficial, like, because you have to be licensed to take bets. Yes, I made a few quid but then I changed my job and didn't see so many people after that. They do say that the only way to make any money from horse racing is to own a racehorse.'

'That's not exactly true, Alan!' Twm called out from his seat at the card table. 'I happen to know someone who owns a racehorse and it just doesn't quite work like that. I'm told you have to be pretty high up in racin' circles to be in the know, and that has its ups and downs too. But I will say this, boys: when the high-ups win, they bluddy win big – and I mean BIG.'

'That reminds me of a horse racing joke, Twm,' said Johnny, his back against the bar. 'This chap was at the racetrack leaning on the rails when one of the local stable lads came up to him and asked him if he would like the winner of the next race. And he said, 'No, thanks. I've only got a small garden!'

The bar erupted with laughter as Johnny, smiling broadly, turned towards the bar and murmured, 'Two pints of best bitter, please, Trefor.'

Chapter 16

Rabbiting in Winter

ANOTHER WEEK HAD passed swiftly in the Plough Inn without anything to gossip about and the usual players were gathered around the big table in the main bar. As ever, a game of four-handed cribbage was in progress. Johnny and Alan were leading their opponents, Colin and Bobby, by more than a dozen holes on the scoreboard.

'Hey, Colin!' Johnny said, as he shuffled the cards in preparation to dealing another hand. 'I haven't yerd anything lately about you getting any rabbits! Have you given up going out hunting for them?'

Colin looked up from under the peak of his cap at the question, wondering if Johnny was serious or pulling his leg as he replied, 'No, you're right enough, Johnny. To tell you the truth, I'm finding it a bit hard to get up a head of steam to go out on my own since my father died. I should make an effort, though, cos those terriers of ours need to work. P'raps I'll take them out for a run pretty soon.'

'Then I'll buy the first rabbit you bring in yere!' Alan interrupted with a short laugh. 'I like a bit of roast rabbit, 'specially with chips, brembutter and a nice cup of tea.'

'Not a chance, Alan. I might want that one for myself. You'll just 'ave to wait an' see, won't you?' Colin placed the nine of diamonds on the board.

'And my six makes fifteen two. Peg two, Alan,' Johnny grinned, as he looked at his playing partner.

'And two for us, Col,' said Bobby, as he placed another six in front of him.

Alan followed that with a ten of hearts to make it thirty-one. 'And two for us, is it?'

'Well, I've only got four. Two pairs. What have you got, Col?'

'Not a bluddy thing. Sorry, Bobby.'

Alan called out, 'I've only got six. Can you better that, Johnny?'

'Well, I think so. I've got ten. So, you've given up hunting foxes, then?'

'I didn't say that, Johnny. I've just got to get a few things sorted out in my head, that's all.'

'Well, when you have working terriers, they have to be kept busy or they will find mischief and destroy anything they can get hold of. I know all about that. Remember that little terrier I bought off your father when he was short of money? Well, I built a big pen for him while I was in work. The little sod would dig his way out of there just about every day, even though I had buried the chicken wire about a foot below ground. In the end I found a way to stop him. I found an old yard brush with really tough bristles, the sort the old road sweepers used. I chopped off the handle to half its length and hammered it into the ground in the middle of his pen until only the very tips were showing above ground. Well, I watched him for a while as he walked around it and then he would jump at it trying to dig it out. He never dug his way out after that. That old brush head kept him busy all day. No more escapes down to the school to run with the kids at playtime. Der, he was a great little dog but he wouldn't listen to my wife when she called him, and got himself run over chasing a cat across the road.'

Colin nodded. 'Cats are crafty animals, mind. I'm sure they've caused a lot of dogs to lose their lives. I've seen some of 'em get away from a pack of dogs by jumpin' as much as 12 feet straight up in the air to the top of a wall when we lived in Waun-gron.'

'Forget the cats, Colin. I want to talk about rabbiting,' Johnny grinned as he picked up the cards and began shuffling them slowly. 'I can remember a few years ago, maybe even further back than that, I went out with my dog and Fred with his dogs. It was just after Christmas, when we had a really heavy frost. It was just like we had snow. The ground was white and we were crossing the *waun* towards Hendre Fawr when Fred put his arm out to stop me going forward. He whispered, "Haisht a minute! See those little tracks by there?" I looked, but all I could see were some smudges in the frost that didn't go anywhere. Fred twttied down and pointed to where the track was wider in one place. "He've jumped sideways, see?" he whispered, holding on to the dogs. He stood up slowly and took the safety off his 16-bore. "Now then, Johnny. Watch the dogs." Suddenly your little Jack Russell, Judy, bolted towards a clump of reeds about 15 feet away and out jumped a bluddy big rabbit. Fred had his gun up in a split second and had him before Judy got to the clump of reeds. Damn, your old man was quick with the gun, Colin.'

'And with his lip,' Trefor called out across the room.

'Aye, that too,' said Johnny. 'All this chopsin' is making me thirsty.' He took a long swig of his beer. 'Who dealt last?'

'I didn't. Must be my turn now,' said Alan, grinning. 'C'mon, *brawd*. Remember there's a pint on this game, mind!'

'Aye, okay. Right then. Enough of Fred and his antics, okay?'

Alan began to deal the cards.

'Aye,' said Colin quietly. 'I still miss the old so and so, mind.' He picked up his cards and played the Jack of Diamonds.

Johnny immediately played a five. 'And two, Alan,' he said.

'And twenty for two,' Bobby said in low tones, matching Johnny's five of hearts.

'And twenty-five for six!' Alan grinned as he placed the third five and pegged another six holes on the scoreboard.

Without saying a word, Colin gathered up the cards and shuffled them quickly, offering them to Alan to cut before dealing the final hand. Alan just tapped the top of the pack and Colin began to deal.

Johnny looked at his watch and said, 'Alan, if we go out on this hand, I'm going to finish playing – if that's okay with you, mind. I think I've had enough cards for tonight.'

'Oh aye, aye. That's okay by me. I could do with a break. Are you on next, Roy?'

'Well, I did knock the board when you were out back, Alan.'

A couple of minutes later the game was over. Johnny stood up and stretched his arms above his head. 'If you don't mind, Col, instead of a fresh pint I'll have a small bottle to liven up the remains of this one?'

'Me, too!' said Alan. 'Is that okay, Bobby? Two small bottles are cheaper than two pints of best bitter. Isn't that right, Tref?'

Trefor shrugged and said, 'Whatever you want, boys.'

'Right then, Tref. Two small bottles of pale ale. Bobby and Colin are paying. So, what's new then? How's your butcher friend treating you these days?'

'Oh, you know. The same old thing. My phone rings about three o'clock in the morning but now I don't even pick it up. I know it's him and I'm pretty sure he'll be as mad as 'ell because I don't answer it. Then he won't be able to go to sleep, thinking about other ways to try and upset me.' He laughed and added, 'If I keep this up and he gets no satisfaction from annoying me, p'raps he'll give up.'

'Not a chance,' said Alan. 'He's that type of bloke.'

Trefor shrugged. 'Well, it doesn't really bother me any more. It did in the beginning, mind, but not now!'

Changing the subject, Johnny remarked, 'I haven't seen Arwyn in yere for a while.'

Willi Bray, all ears a few feet away while waiting to be served, chipped in. 'That's cos he's had a bit of a pull and hasn't been out of the farmhouse for the past three weeks or so.'

'And how do you come to know that, Willi?' Trefor asked politely as he placed the foaming pint in front of him, at the same time holding out his hand for payment.

'Somebody from the farm was saying about it in the Co-op last week and my wife yerd them talking about it, that's all.'

Johnny and Alan, grinning, nodded knowingly to each other. It appeared Mr Nosy Parker was still in top form.

'Oh, is that so? Do you know what ails him, Willi? Trefor smiled and winked at the two councillors, who were grinning like Cheshire Cats.

'No, I don't, only that he hasn't been well. Sorry, boys.'

As if by magic, the bar door opened slowly and the tall, avuncular figure of Arwyn limped into the room. 'Evening, boys,' he murmured, smiling weakly at the concerned sea of faces staring at him. 'What's wrong with you boys? You all look like you've seen a bluddy ghost or something!'

'No, no, nothing like that!' Trefor said hastily, breaking the sudden silence. 'We were this very minute talking about you and we were told that you hadn't been very well, mun.'

Arwyn looked slowly around the room and laughed. 'So, you were told I was not well, eh? Well, I think I know who that would be, without me pointing a finger. Well, yere I am and I'm not a bluddy ghost, boys. Trefor, gimme a pint of best bitter before I die of thirst! I haven't had a pint in more than three weeks now. Aye, boys – I've been laid up for more than three weeks after one of my young rams charged into me.'

'Never!' said Trefor, a shocked look on his round features. A few of the older regulars came up to the bar to shake Arwyn by the hand.

'Aye, boys. I had all my rams in a tidy-sized pen cos I was going to get the vet to have a look at them before I turned them loose in my top fields, when I noticed one of them had a bit of a limp. I got in there amongst them when all of a sudden, this bluddy young ram charged at me from the side and butted me right on my knee joint and down I went. Lucky for me, one of my boys was on the other side of the pen and jumped in to help me up. When the doctor came up from Waun-gron he said to rest my knee, but I might have to have surgery if it don't get better on its own. He said the ligaments in my bluddy knee had been damaged, or whatever. BUT yere I am, as large as life, to have a pint with the boys. So, let's have it, Tref!'

'And a pint of best bitter you shall have, Arwyn!' Trefor grabbed a pint glass and, filling it to the brim, he placed it in front of him. 'Yere you are, Mr Davies. A pint of best bitter at no charge.'

Arwyn, nodding his head in thanks, lifted the honey-coloured liquid to his lips and said '*Iechyd da*, Trefor.' He raised the glass and smacked his lips as he savoured that familiar bitter taste.

'So, what's new, boys? Have I missed anything important?'

'Not a thing, Arwyn,' Johnny replied, looking up at the tall farmer.

Arwyn grinned and said, 'Well, there's three weeks out of my life I didn't use, but I'm glad that I didn't miss anything I could have made a fuss over.'

Alan picked up his pint, swirled the remains in the bottom, and downed it in one go. 'Well, boys, that's all for me tonight. I've got to be in work early in the morning. So, I'll bid you all goodnight. Nice to see you about, Arwyn. See you tomorrow, Johnny. Hey, Colin! Don't forget about that rabbit for me!'

CHAPTER 17

Blackout at the Mount

OLD JOHN SHINKINS rose from his usual seat on the wooden settle beside the stove. He tucked his ancient grey woollen muffler down the front of his equally ancient, leather-buttoned cardigan as he made his way across the room to the bar.

'Pint please, Trefor.'

'Certainly, John.' Trefor smiled in reply, and then asked, 'So, what's new, then, down on the council estate?'

Old John gave a sniff of disdain and looked at his pocket watch comparing the time with the large clock on the wall behind the landlord.

'Nothing of importance, Tref. Mind you, I don't go out much to get any *clecs* these days. I know,' he held up a gnarled hand. 'I do come yere every day and most nights but,' he turned to look around the bar, 'this is where I hear all the local gossip, same as you. Mind you, I still hear a lot of stories about Fred Howells and his antics, even though he's been gone quite a while now.'

Trefor nodded in agreement. 'Yes, John *bach*, I hear them all the time – and I do miss his old nonsense, especially in yere with all the boys and him, having fun. I remember the time when him and Colin were living in the Mount Cottage and some of the boys were winding him up about going rabbiting. They wanted to go early the following morning to somewhere over in Breconshire. It was some place only he knew about and had been bragging about all night.'

'Funny, but I don't remember that one, Tref!'

'Aye, you do! I remember Jimmy sitting by you over there and doing his best to get Fred going. He'd had a few pints by then, mind, and Colin kept telling his father to leave it there, Daddy! Of course, Fred wasn't one to listen to any sort of good advice from anybody, was he? Anyway, Jimmy and Titch and a few others kept on at Fred until he finally agreed to leave for Brecon in George Teale's car at five o'clock the following morning, which was a Saturday and none of them were working. After getting Fred to agree, Jimmy wanted to put money on it that Fred wouldn't show up, because he wouldn't be able to get out of bed at that time in the morning. Fred, as usual, took the bait hook, line and sinker.'

'"Won't I, by damn! We'll see about that, Jimmy," he said, with some of his old temper boiling up as he went on. "I'll tell you what then, Jimmy! I'll bet you ten bluddy pints that I'll be on the front step at five o'clock in the morning, waiting for you lot to show up!"'

'And was he there on time, Tref?' Old John took a long swig of his beer.

'Not by a long shot, John. Jimmy, Titch, Georgie Teale and I think a few others went over to the Mount long after closing when they thought that Fred and Colin would be fast asleep. Quietly, they pinned black bin bags over every window and door, then ran off into the night. It turned out that Fred and Colin didn't get out of bed until late in the afternoon when Fred got up to go to the toilet out the back. Fred, by all accounts, was tampin'! He was thinking that he now owed Jimmy ten pints! He still thought that until he came in yere later and Jimmy, fair play, confessed. And, fair play to Fred too, he had a bluddy good laugh about it.'

'Well, Trefor, I must be getting old cos I don't remember that one at all.' Old John was leaning back against the bar, weak from laughing and struggling to get his breath back.

After a while he straightened up, still holding onto the edge of the bar, and said, 'You know, Trefor, there's nothing too hot for some of these boys coming yere and that's the truth. Sometimes it's not safe to turn your bluddy back on them. Although I have to say, that was a real good one and there was no harm in it, was there?'

He took another swig from his pint and walked slowly back to his seat. From there he could oversee the continuing game of crib. A few minutes went by as he thought again about Fred and some of his outrageous antics over the many years that he had known him living down in Waun-gron. On the spur of the moment he called out, 'Hey, Colin! I was just reminded by Trefor of the time some of the boys pinned black plastic bags over the windows, when you lived in the Mount Cottage!'

Colin glanced towards Old John. 'Aye, the rotten sods. I slept so 'ard, boys, I was tired out! Yes, John. I remember that one very well. Jimmy and the boys really 'ad us. They thought it was pretty clever to 'ave everyone laughin' at me and Fred. But not many people know we had our own back on Jimmy and Georgie a few weeks later. I'll bet any money you like, they never told anyone about that!'

'Well, go on then, Colin! It's water under the bridge now!'

Old John got to his feet and shuffled a bit closer to the card table. He didn't want to miss anything that Colin might reveal about their payback.

Colin was silent for a few moments then with a short laugh he said, 'Well, we'd yerd a whisper somewhere that Jimmy and George 'ad asked the local squire for permission to 'unt vermin on his land, cos he'd let his gamekeeper take some time off as his father was pretty low at his 'ome near Hereford. So we'd gone there on this particular day pretty early and told the man at the gatehouse we were Jimmy and George. That morning, we managed to bag a dozen rabbits in no time at all. Fred cleaned them pretty quick and we bolted out of there before they showed up. We then went down to Waun-gron and sold the rabbits to one of the butchers Fred knew from when we lived down there. You know Llew Lewis, don't you, John?'

'Oh, aye, I know him all right.' Old John nodded, holding on the back of Roy's chair for support. 'Aye, I know him very well. We used to buy meat from him too.'

'Well, we sold all those rabbits for five bob each and on the strength of that money we called in the Globe and 'ad a few before catchin' the bus home. So in the end we 'ad the last laugh, John – but that was ages and ages ago. Right, boys! Where are we with this game, then?'

'If you want to know, we are all sitting yere like dummies waiting for you to finish bragging about your little trick on Jimmy and George Teale,' Bobby replied, grinning like the Cheshire Cat.

Colin sighed. 'I wasn't bluddy braggin', Bobby. I was puttin' the record straight, that's all, cos one way or another me and my father always seemed to be in it. Right, boys?' He looked at the others seated around the table for confirmation.

'You're right enough, Colin. But I think a lot of that was Fred's own fault, wasn't it?' said Old John. 'Remember, I knew your father before you were born and he was the same then and nothing in the world would ever change 'im. Sorry, Colin.' He turned away to shuffle back to his seat without another word.

'Okay, boys!' Twm raised his voice. 'That's enough! Are we playing cards or not?'

'We are playing cards!' Bobby replied, straight-faced.

'Okay by me,' Colin added, playing the nine of clubs.

'Fifteen for two,' said Roy, putting the six of hearts down on the board.

Johnny, Alan and Trefor, at the far end of the room, looked at each other and shrugged.

'Another storm in a teacup,' Trefor murmured with a smile. 'And old Fred is not even yere. That's what I like about this place. Everyone knows everybody else's business and they are all okay with that.'

'Aye,' Alan said laughing. 'And there's a few around yere who want to mind everybody's else's business too!'

'C'mon Alan,' Johnny cut in, joining in the laughter. 'You mustn't talk about poor Willi Bray like that when he's not yere to defend himself and deny he's nosy.' He paused, the smile on his face fading. 'Hey! That reminds me of a joke I yerd the other day. Owen's wife said her husband is a bit nosy. Well, she didn't actually tell him that. He read about it in her diary. Boom boom!'

'Yes, an oldie but a goody,' said Trefor smiling. 'Those are always the best.'

Chapter 18

Giant Rabbits

'Hey, Colin! I've been meaning to ask you for a long time now!' Old John Shinkins called out the second he came into the bar.

'And what's that, Mr Shinkins?' Colin turned to face him, at the same time calling out, 'A pint of best bitter if you please, Trefor! What's that then, John?'

'Aye, what happened to those whopping rabbits your father bought for breeding? If I remember, he was all for it and bragging how much money he was going to make off them.'

'Oh, them things,' Colin replied, walking slowly towards the card table and taking a swig from his pint as he sat down. 'To tell you the truth, John *bach*, I don't know where he got 'em or even if he bought 'em. Yes, he 'ad that idea for a long time – to get some rabbits and breed from 'em for sale as pets – so he built a big pen for 'em at the bottom of our garden. That was empty for almost two years and the grass in there was about a foot high so there would be plenty of food for 'em when he got around to getting some.

'Then one day, right out of the blue, he just came 'ome with two large baskets. He told me he 'ad just come from Waun-gron and showed me these two yuge rabbits. Boys, I 'ad never seen anythin' that big in my life and I must 'ave shot 'undreds of bluddy rabbits. Well, Fred put the two of 'em in the pen and said, "All we 'ave to do now, Colin, is wait." And wait he did, cos months and months went by with nothin' 'appening. Fred used to sit on a chair out the back and watch 'em chasin' each other around the bluddy pen and still nothin' 'appened.

'Then one day a chap from Waun-gron called Charlie Hopkins came to the 'ouse with a lovely little terrier. He wanted to know if Fred would like to buy 'im. Fair play, Fred 'ad a good look at 'im but in the end he said, "No, thanks. This one is more of a lovely pet and would be too kind for 'unting foxes." Then this chap Charlie went over to the rabbits' pen and said, "Years ago I used to keep rabbits and show them in competitions, and I won a few cups too. What are you doing with these Flemish Giants yere, then?"

'Fred looked at 'im a bit *twp*. "What do you mean, Charlie? What Giants?"

'"That's the name of this breed of rabbit, Fred. These can weigh as much as 20 lb and grow to about two and a half feet long. These two are not mature yet. In the very beginning, these animals were bred only for their meat and fur."

'"Oh," he said, "I was thinking of breeding from 'em and selling 'em as pets to the pet shops in Aberdare, Merthyr and p'raps Neath. I thought it was a good idea to make a few bob on the side."

'But Charlie just laughed at 'im and said, "Not from these two you won't, Fred, unless you get a buck to go in with them."

'Fred looked at 'im, his mouth open. "What are you talking about, Charlie?"

'"By my reckoning, Fred, just looking at the shape of their heads, these are two does. The male of this breed is much larger and can weigh up to 25 lb. That's a lot of rabbit, mind. Do you want me to take a look to make sure that what I'm telling you is right?"

'"Aye, Charlie, if you wouldn't mind," says my dad.

'Then Charlie lifted the top off the pen, climbed in, and grabbed one of the rabbits. In seconds he told my father, "Fred, I'm right enough, these are both young does." He started laughin' and told my father he would be waitin' for a very long time for these two to produce a litter.

'I remember my father takin' off his cap and throwin' it 'alfway across the garden in temper as he shouted out, "Those bluddy gypsies caught me, then!" Charlie then asked my father how much he'd paid for them.

'"Huh? Oh, I gave this chap three flagons of best bitter for both of them in two wicker baskets."

'Charlie said, "I don't think that was such a bad deal, Fred. All you have to do now is buy a buck of the same breed. Any other buck, these would kill it right away. Besides, you said they came in two wicker baskets? They must be worth more than a few shillings each, cos the gypsies make some really good baskets."

'My father grudgingly agreed with 'im about the baskets but he said that they'd lied to 'im about 'em bein' a pair for breedin'. Then Charlie told 'im that it wasn't a problem, as he climbed out of the pen and put the top back on. He said, "If you like Fred, I'll 'ave a look through my old records to see if I can find someone who's still breeding these Flemish Giants and let you know."

'Oh, my father was pleased about that, John. He said, "Aye? That's good of you, Charlie. Thanks for that." Then he looked again at the little terrier, sittin' quietly watchin' the two rabbits chasin' each other around the pen, and said, "Damn, Charlie! That's a pretty little dog, mind, but I don't think he is one for me. Sorry about that."

'Charlie said it wasn't a problem. He clipped the lead on the dog's collar and said, "I won't bother with the old bus. I think I'll take a little stroll back to Waun-gron now." He shook 'ands with Fred and disappeared around the corner of our 'ouse and that's the last we saw of Charlie Hopkins.

'Yes, John, I can tell you Fred was down in the dumps after Charlie left. He went to sit on the chair out the back, lookin' beyond the 'edge at the bottom of the garden – just starin' up at the Forestry and Craig y Llyn. He seemed to be lost in a world of his own and wasn't like my father at all, was it? He sat there fr'ages, mutterin': "I've got two bluddy does, by damn."'

'True enough, Colin. Not a bit like I remember him,' Old John nodded.

'Anyway, boys, my father kept those two rabbits for another six months or so but never found anyone with a buck to sell 'im. Then one day, we didn't 'ave a scrap of food in the 'ouse and Fred was flat broke…'

'As usual,' Trefor called out across the room.

'Aye, as usual,' Colin said agreeably, then raised his voice. 'Sometimes it 'appens to us all, Trefor.' There were murmurs of agreement to that. 'As I was sayin', boys – we didn't 'ave a scrap of food in the 'ouse and we were both bluddy starvin'. Fred was lookin' out of the kitchen window and I suppose he could see those two rabbits, and they were bluddy yuge by this time. Well, on the spur of the moment, he went out there and killed one of them, just like that.' Colin snapped his fingers. 'It was all a bit sudden but we 'ad 'ell of a feed from the meat on it. I know I've shot 'undreds of wild rabbits, but this seemed to be a bit cruel, like killin' a pet, cos we'd been feedin' them a few bits and pieces for months. But there you are, Charlie told Fred that in the past they 'ad been bred for meat and by damn he was right. Boys, that was the best-tastin' rabbit I'd ever 'ad in my life, and it tastes even better when you 'ave an empty belly.'

Old John leaned forward, his hand on the back of Bobby's chair for support. 'And what about the other one, Colin. Did you eat that one too?'

'Aye, we did, John, but months later. And I 'ave to say: it didn't taste anythin' like as good as that first one. To me, anyway.'

Everyone around the table and beyond began laughing at Colin's serious tone of voice and his taste for rabbit meat.

To add to the fun, Trefor called out, 'So, what's on the menu next, then, Colin?'

'I dunno! Whatever I can scrounge up, I suppose. Remember me tellin' you boys a long time ago how I got used to 'unting for food in our 'ouse when my father was alive and we were livin' together up on the Bryn? Well, I wish he was still around cos I still miss the old so and so.'

CHAPTER 19

Fishing for Chickens

'HEY, TREFOR, LISTEN!' Twm wiped the froth from his mouth with the back of his hand and put his almost empty pint glass back on the table. 'I've just come from the New Inn and the new bloke over there has just started serving chicken and chips in a basket. You can have that and a pint for just six bob! What are you going to put on yere, then?'

'Twm *bach*, I can't ever see me doing anything like that. This is a working man's pub and I am quite happy to sell a couple of barrels of beer a week to all you boys. Be fair, Twm, where else would you go to have as much fun as goes on in yere? You won't find anything like this in the New Inn, will you?'

Colin, sitting opposite Twm, began shuffling the pack of cards, ready to deal the next hand. 'Talkin' of chicken! Der, my father was 'ell of a boy, as we all know, but listen to this one. I remember comin' 'ome from work one afternoon and he was sittin' by the fire reading a week-old *Aberdare Leader*. I said, "Daddy, I'm bluddy starvin'. What's for grub tonight?"

'From behind the paper he said, "Same as usual, sod all. Although," he added, "I'm tellin' a fib, Colin. I've still got some spuds and onions in the ground at the bottom of the garden."

'So I said, "It'd be 'andy if we had a chicken to go with 'em!"

'Well, Fred lowered the paper and said, "Colin, you are forever giving me brilliant ideas!"

'I 'ad no idea what he was on about. Next thing, he jumped up out of his chair and said, "C'mon, Col! Let's go fishing for some chickens for our supper, is it?" He's gone now so it doesn't matter who knows what he did that night.'

'What the 'ell are you talking about, Colin?' Alan asked from across the table. 'Fishing for chickens?'

Colin laughed and pushed his cap a bit further back on his head. 'That's exactly what I'm talkin' about, Alan. About four or p'raps five years ago, me and Fred were comin' back from 'Skelta' (Ystradfellte to you) and we came down into the Bont behind the Angel pub. Then, as we crossed the Nedd by the old bridge, Fred spotted a fishin' rod, lyin' in the grass by the road. It was a green-coloured rod and we thought at the time that someone with a car 'ad put it on the ground and forgot about it. So, Fred picked it up and we made our way yere up Pencaedrain Road. You must know the one – it comes out by the Don Café.

'Anyway, on this particular day he went to the cwtch under the stairs and brought out that rod, at the same time tellin' me, "This is what we need, Col. C'mon, let's go down to Waun-gron right away, is it?"

'Boys, just before you come into Waun-gron on the right-hand side of the A465, there's a yuge chicken farm. I can't remember the name of it at the moment, but that doesn't matter, does it? Anyway, it's the farm right below the Nant Hir reservoir, and when the owner, Tomos Davies, cleared the land, he left a big tump of dirt almost by the road. Over the years a lot of bushes grew there, and that's where we cwtched to watch his chickens behind this 10-foot chain-link fence. He got all that fencin' for nothin', so Fred said, from the old wartime factories yere in Rhyd-y-groes.

'Anyway, we sat there fr'ages, until 'alf a dozen of Twm's Buff Orpingtons came close to the fence. Fred 'ad dug up a big juicy worm, which he put on the 'ook and then he cast the line over the fence. Like a flash, one of them 'ens grabbed it and Fred yanked on the line a bit sharpish. Next minute he was reelin' it in and the bird was pulled up the fence by the 'ook in its beak. In less than a minute Fred 'ad 'old of it and 'ad wrung its neck.

'"What about that then, Colin?" he said. "Well, it looks OK, but remember Daddy, this is like stealing, mind!" I replied. "Not really, Colin. Remember last year, when I was working in the Tower Colliery, just up by there?" He nodded in the direction of the distant lights at the bottom of the mountain to the south of where we were. "I put in a full day's work putting in posts for that old skinflint and I never got paid. He kept saying, "I'll pay you tomorrow," but he never did. So, this is like a sort of payment in kind."

'He took the 'ook from its beak and put another worm on it and pitched it over the bluddy fence again, sayin', "We might as well be done for two as one – interest on the pay I didn't get." I picked up the first one – it must 'ave weighed about 7 or 8 lb. He got the second 'en the same way, so within five minutes we were on our way 'ome with Fred cwtchin' the two birds under his big coat.

'We came back over the fields behind Dai Glwyd's place, over the Treherbert road and behind Cynlas Farm and Bryngolwg Farm. By that time it was gettin' dark, so we got 'ome without seein' anybody. Damn, we 'ad a bluddy good feed off those birds that night and for quite a few days after. I told 'im that I'd never yerd of anybody goin' fishin' like that before and do you know what he said? "Colin, it's a little trick I yerd about a long, long time ago."

Everyone around the table had begun laughing at the seriousness in Colin's voice when Alan thumped the table with the side of his fist and raising his voice he said, 'And you expect us to believe that cock and bull story about fishing for chickens? You should go to the top of the class for tall-story telling, Colin. You can get away from yere with that one!'

Some more laughter followed Alan's challenge of the truth in Colin's far-fetched fishing tale, but Colin was adamant. 'I don't care what you say or think, boys. I only know that I enjoyed the taste of those plump chickens. Okay! Let's play cards then!'

Alan and Johnny entered the bar in the Plough the following Tuesday evening and were surprised to find they were the only customers.

'Hello, Tref! Where is everybody?'

'Oh, hello, boys. A lot 'ave been yere early but they've all gone down to the Legion to watch our team play in the Darts Finals of the league in Waun-gron. Did you boys forget it was on tonight?'

'Damn it all, Tref! I've been so busy with different things since last week it went right off the top of my mind – and clearly yours too, is it, Al?'

Alan shrugged and glanced at his watch. 'It's still early, Johnny. We can have a swift half yere and still make it in time. Two bottles of light ale, Tref, and then we'll be on our way!'

As they entered the Legion, the doorman asked them who they were supporting this season.

'Supporting? What are you talking about?' Alan asked with a smile. 'Neath Rugby Club, that's who. Why do you ask?'

'I'm not talking about rugby! It's darts I'm talking about yere! Tonight's the finals, mun!'

'In that case,' Johnny cut in, 'we're yere to support the team from the Plough Inn, Rhyd-y-groes.'

They quickly scribbled their names in the visitors' book and pushed through the double doors to get into the main hall. At that moment, Twm was walking towards the oche and the crowd in the hall went quiet.

It only took a single dart into the double six and the crowd erupted. The Plough Inn had beaten the best in the league to take the Cup and become Champions for the first time.

Twm, all smiles, was surrounded by his teammates, who were all doing their best to thump every scrap of breath from his body by slapping him as hard as they could on his back. Returning to the Plough in high spirits, and waving the League Cup at every opportunity, the team and their supporters entered the bar to cheers from the few regulars who had arrived since Alan and Johhny had left, as they spotted the trophy.

Trefor, his round features wreathed in smiles, stood behind the bar waving a white bar towel and shouting out their names above the clamour.

'Boys! Boys! Bring the team over yere! There are six pints of best bitter lined up waiting for you. Hey, Twm! How many reserves did you have with you tonight, then?'

'Just one, Trefor. Same one as usual, every week!'

'Okay, then. I'll pull another pint for Mr Hopkins. Well done, boys! Very well done! Gimme the Cup and I'll fill it to the brim.' He turned to see the smiling faces of Johnny and Alan. 'Well, boys. This has the makings of another good night in yere, innit?'

'You're right enough there, Trefor. This is their first good win and they've got the League Cup to prove it. It looks like you'll have to make more room on that glass shelf! There'll be no holding these boys now!'

'I don't care, Johnny,' Trefor replied laughing. 'I think this will bring me a lot of business after this!' He turned to look at the narrow glass shelf. 'P'raps I'll have to get a wider one now, cos that Cup's too big to fit on there, innit?'

'Yes, Tref, and I think you might have to dish out a lot of free beer too.'

Trefor paused in the midst of pouring a pint bottle of Evan Evans Bevan's pale ale for Dai Banwen. 'You may very well be right about that, Alan, but I don't think that will matter very much, do you?'

'No! Not for a landlord as rich as you are, anyway!'

Trefor gave a slight smile, without replying to Alan's reference to his alleged family fortune.

'Well, Tref, if this row keeps up, as I'm sure it will, it will no doubt cut into your sleeping time!'

'Aye, Johnny, I'm just as sure you're right about that – but if that bluddy butcher is true to form, he'll be on the phone to this number at 3 a.m. again, anyway.'

'No! He's still up to his old nonsense, then?'

'Well, of course he is! I don't expect him to do anything different now.'

'And I can't understand why you don't go to the police about him, since you know very well who it is. Surely, they can speak to the GPO on your behalf?' Johnny shook his head. 'I know I would be there like a flash to do something about it, but that's me!' He grinned and shrugged his broad shoulders.

'Yes, yes! You've told me that before and I did speak with the Inspector in Aberdare and he said there wasn't much they could really do about it. He did ask me to consider changing my number but I can't be bothered with the potch of doing that.' He had a crafty smile on his round features as he said, 'Besides, it always seems to give me a bit of inspiration to find new ways to catch 'im out and make 'im look a *twpsyn* in front of everybody. I'm pleased to say that I've done this – as you boys know – time after time, but he never learns from it, does he?'

Trefor beamed as Johnny and Alan began to laugh out loud.

'Trefor, I like the way you think,' said Johnny.

'Haisht a minute, Johnny, not so loud. We don't want everybody to know that, do we?'

Trefor looked up as three of the darts team, still savouring the free beer, moved closer to Alan and Johnny and one of them spoke directly to Trefor.

'Listen, Tref: it looks like we've got a winning team yere at last. So, comin back yere in the car, us boys had a bit of a chat. We was thinking now of joining the Aberdare Darts League and the one down there in Glynneath next season and…' he paused, 'I have been nominated to ask if you will sponsor us from now on.'

Johnny and Alan looked at each other and pulled a face, as if to say, 'There's posh'.

Trefor looked at the team spokesman with a smile. 'Sponsor you? What exactly do you mean – "sponsor" you?'

'Well, you know – you'd be the big shot behind the Plough Inn team.'

Trefor raised his bushy eyebrows in surprise. 'Be the big shot, is it? And what will that cost me, Terry?'

'Not much, I shouldn't think,' Terry replied with a grin. 'You must know we're going to bring a lot of business to this pub if we're in the other leagues, because we'd then be playing three nights a week – and that's without counting the practice nights we'd be yere too.'

'Yes!' Johnny cut in before Trefor could reply. 'That is, if your wives and or girlfriends will let you out of their sight for all that time! Boys, you have to think about them, mind.'

Terry turned to face them. 'Thanks for that, boys!' he answered, the smile on his face fading rapidly as he grudgingly admitted. 'Well, there is that too, I s'pose. Anyway, as I was saying. We will need a bit of backing and we thought that you Trefor, as landlord of our pub, would like to help us out?'

Trefor leaned on the bar with his forearms and clasped his meaty hands together. He looked speculatively at the three delegates and then said, 'I'll give your request my serious consideration, boys, and that's the best I can do tonight, okay?

Now go and join your teammates and enjoy the rest of the night.' He straightened up and placed a pint in front of each of them without asking for payment.

Terry and the others nodded their thanks, then Trefor signalled them to come closer and spoke quietly to them. Then Terry said, 'Fair enough, Tref. We'll talk to you again when we haven't had any beer and,' he waved a hand in the direction of the noise, 'when it's a bit quieter in yere.' They picked up their pints and moved across the room to join the crowd around the cup.

Trefor turned towards Alan and Johnny. 'So, what do you think about that, then, boys?'

'To me, it doesn't sound like a bad idea at all, Tref. If they can get away with it on the home front and play yere three nights a week, it could be very good for business in yere, for the darts season, anyway.'

'It all sounds okay in theory,' said Alan, 'but – and it's a big but – what if they can't get accepted in either the Aberdare or Glynneath leagues? And, on top of that, as you mentioned earlier, Johnny, would the women put up with it? Also, it sounds like a lot of spending to me.'

'Yes...' Trefor turned away to pull a pint for Willi Bray. Willi looked from Trefor to the two councillors and asked, 'So, what's going on then, boys? This is part of tonight's celebration, is it?'

Johnny smiled. 'Heck no, Willi. This has nothing to do with that,' he replied, nodding towards the crowd at the other end of the bar.

As Willi walked away, disappointed at not knowing what they had been discussing, Johnny nudged Alan and whispered, 'Look at Trefor, Al. You can almost see his mind ticking over as he calculates how much this darts team will bring into the Plough.'

Moments later, Trefor came back to where they were standing and Johnny said, 'I have an idea for you to consider, Tref.

To sponsor a team, it would have to be something tangible. I was thinking it might be a good idea to have, say, a few dozen T-shirts made up in red or black, with "Plough Inn, Rhyd-y-groes" on the back and "League Champions" across the front. That would be great advertising for this place, don't you think?'

Deep in thought, Trefor looked distantly across the bar. 'Yes, boys. That might be a good idea. I'll find out a bit more when I speak to Terry and the others later this coming week. Yes,' he repeated, as if to himself. 'That's a very good idea indeed. Thank you, boys.'

CHAPTER 20

Beer

O NE SUNDAY MORNING, the usual crowd had gathered around the big table in the Plough Inn for the customary pint or two before lunch. As usually happened in the Plough, comments were passed on the quality and selection of beers available in Trefor's pub.

Twm sat back in his chair, raised his pint towards the bright overhead light and said, 'Boys, just look at this, will you? I'll go as far as to say that the best bitter in this pub is the best bluddy pint you can get anywhere. Am I right, or what?'

There were murmurs of assent all around the table.

Trefor, listening to Twm's statement, beamed as he pulled a pint of the honey-coloured liquid for Old John Shinkins, who had made his daily trek up the long hill from the council estate.

'Yere you are, John *bach*,' he said with a smile. 'Today there's no charge for you on this one.'

Old John's lined features lit up with delight as he wondered why he was on the receiving end of this liquid bounty. 'Oh! *Diolch yn fawr iawn*, Trefor!' he replied in his first language. He raised the pint to his lips and bowed his head slightly in Trefor's direction. He turned and made his way slowly back to his chosen seat on the settle alongside the stove.

'I wonder what has put Trefor in such a generous mood this Sunday morning?' he thought. 'Could be the boys winning the

League last night, or it could be something that nobody knows about yet.' He sniffed. 'I'll just enjoy the free beer, is it?' He looked across the room at Twm, Roy, Colin and Bobby joking around as they got ready to play another hand of crib. 'Yes,' he thought, 'there's a lot of fun in yere today.'

Colin started speaking in a voice loud enough for Trefor and everyone else in the room to hear. 'Boys, talkin' of beer, Fred reckoned there's no such thing as bad beer. He said, "It's just that some beer is a lot better than others." Anyway, one day me and Fred went to Aberdare cos he'd read in the *Aberdare Leader* that the Corn Stores, that's the one by Rosie's Café, was sellin' a special dog food cheap. The paper said it would make the bones of pups stronger. To this day, I don't know if that was true or not, but Fred wanted to know a bit more about it. While we were in that street, we went into Capanini's for a bag of chips. Der, they make good chips...'

'Hey, Colin! When are you going to get to the bluddy story?'

'Oh, aye! I was forgettin'. Well, me and Fred went into one of those backstreet pubs. I can't remember the name of it now but it was a dingy place. Fred asked this grumpy-lookin' woman behind the bar for two pints. Well, boys, you should 'ave seen. It looked a bit cloudy even in the dim light. Just like 'omemade scrumpy. Fred 'eld the glass up to the light, tasted it and pulled a face. He asked her to please change it for somethin' else. She wanted to know what was wrong with the beer. He said he thought it was a bit off and it tasted like vinegar. She said, "That can't be, because it's a fresh barrel." So Fred told her that when he looked that bad, his mother 'ad sat up all night with 'im.'

The crowd in the bar erupted in laughter while Colin did his best to keep a straight face, but in the end he couldn't stop himself joining in with them.

'Aye,' he said. 'My father was 'ell of a boy, mind. Yere's another little story to show what he was like. We were walkin' down through Cwm Hendre Fawr with the dogs and shotguns when we saw this chap sleepin' under the 'edge. Well, Fred made some sort of noise and he woke up with a frightened look on his face when he saw us standin' there with our guns under our arms. He put his 'ands in the air right away until Fred told 'im he was okay. Then for some reason Fred went over, put his 16-bore on the grass and sat down beside 'im, which I thought was a bit funny, and started talking to 'im. This chap was about Fred's age or p'raps a bit older. He 'ad long grey 'air down to his shoulders and was wearing a heavy army overcoat. It 'ad an old badge on it but I didn't know what it was.

'Now yere's a funny thing. Our two dogs went straight over to him and cwtched in by his legs. I found that a bit strange, too, because our Glen of Imaal terrier, Rose, would not go to strangers. So, while Fred and 'im were chatting, I went to sit on the bank to 'ave a smoke.

'We never went any further down the Cwm cos Fred said it was time for a pint, so we walked back to the Plough. Fred told me later that this chap 'ad spent some time in Borstal cos he'd "borrowed" a bike to go to work. He said the people there 'ad beaten 'im up and locked 'im in a cell and he swore then that once he got out of there he would never stay inside a building ever again. He was in the army when the war started and said he was lucky to be alive cos he'd seen some awful things.

'Fred told me he'd asked this chap, Joe – that was 'is name – about work and what he could do. He said he loved to work on a farm and he was pretty good at everything. Fred told him he knew a lot of farmers in the area and he would try and get him some work, and he did too.

'This chap Joe would work for a few hours at each of the farms all over the place. I was told that he didn't want to sleep inside on a proper bed. Instead he said he liked to sleep out in the open somewhere. He was a bit of a strange bloke but he got on with everybody on the farms. Ned Hopkins told me he was out pickin' mushrooms early one mornin' and found 'im sleepin', sittin' up in a wheelbarrow. He'd tipped it up so the 'andles were on the ground and he 'ad a big grain sack in the barrow and was fast asleep in the corner of an open barn out in the fields. Funny sort of a chap, but he was all right, I suppose.'

Johnny picked up the pack of cards and began to shuffle them. 'So, what was this chap's name then, Col?'

'I told you earlier, boys. He was called Joe – but I don't know if that was his real name. That was the name he gave us, so Fred called 'im Bristol Joe cos that's where he said he came from. I remember he 'ad this funny accent, though.'

'So where is this story going, then, Col?' Twm asked as he put his hand in order before playing the first card.

'Oh! Well, Joe 'ad some clever little tricks. He 'ad a 'omemade catapult that he used to knock pigeons off their perch using steel ball bearings. You can't eat many of those in a week cos they'll bluddy kill you. I read that somewhere.

'I saw him in the Globe in Waun-gron one afternoon throwin' his 'omemade darts. They looked a bit like 'orseshoe nails but by damn he could throw them. He 'ad one of the old men to 'old an empty flagon bottle against the dartboard and he threw those three darts right into the bottle. Aye, right down the neck! The landlord got a bit annoyed after, because they 'ad to break the bluddy bottle to get his darts back! That was some trick, but when the landlord came from behind the bar, he suddenly cleared off. To this day I've never seen 'im again.'

'He sounds like someone we need for the Plough darts team, innit?' Twm said, looking around for confirmation.

'I don't think so, Twm. He's not around yere anymore – or p'raps he's passed away under a hedge or something, who knows?' Colin raised his voice. 'Has anyone seen any sign of Bristol Joe?' A chorus of 'No' came back to him.

'Okay, boys! That's enough of my tales for one night. Cut the cards, Roy, and let's get this game going. Oh – I just remembered something else. He 'ad a knack for pickin' winners at the track and Fred jumped on that one right away. So it's no wonder he was always ready to sit down and have a chat with 'im.'

'One time there was a trip goin' from Waun-gron to the track at Chepstow races. Fred managed to get enough cash together to go with 'em. Georgie Whatsisname from Manchester Place in Waun-gron told us a little story about Fred at the track, and his bettin' system. Fred never told me, mind!'

'What bluddy betting system?' Roy said with a laugh. 'Your father lost more "winners" than he would ever let on.'

'Wait on, Roy!' Alan interrupted, grinning. 'Let's hear these *clecs* from that Chepstow trip, is it?'

'Aye, boys, you 'ave to listen to this one. Fred was down by the rails with the boys from Manchester Place and the jockeys were walkin' their nags up the 'ill to the start. Fred was all eyes cos he'd never been this close to any racehorses before. Georgie said that Fred turned to 'im and said 'ow beautiful the animals were. Then he said, "See that number 6 'orse? If he turns and looks at me and nods his 'ead at me, I'm going to put five bob on 'im to win." Georgie told me the bluddy 'orse did exactly as Fred said it would. Fred was off like a shot to put his five bob with the nearest bookie.'

'And did the horse win the race?' asked Alan, winking at the other players.

'Nah! I think it came in last and there were only five runners in that race. Anyway, that was the story, accordin' to Georgie Whatsisname.'

The crowd around the table, enjoying the telling of Fred's antics at the racecourse, began laughing. Roy raised his hands in the air and said, 'There you are, boys! That was Fred all over, wasn't it?'

CHAPTER 21

Conkers for Sale

D AI BANWEN ENTERED the Plough and looked around the bar. The usual regulars were all there. Johnny and Alan were at the farmhouse table playing four-handed crib against Twm and Roy. Colin and Bobby were waiting in the wings to play next, while the crowd around the table included Will Mawr, Willi Bray, the tall figure of Arwyn and the farmer from Hendre Fawr. Dai nodded towards Old John Shinkins – seated in his usual spot on the wooden settle, from which he could watch the progress of the card game – and walked over to the bar, where Trefor was busily polishing some pint glasses he had just washed.

'Pint bottle, please, Tref.'

'Right away, Mr Jones,' said Trefor, light-heartedly formal. Jones was Dai's real surname but everyone who knew him called him Dai Banwen.

Trefor poured Dai's favourite bottle of Evan Evans Bevan's ale and asked him if he had any news. This was one of the ways that Trefor, working long hours in the pub, kept up with local gossip and events.

Dai took a swig of the bubbling ale and smacked his lips with satisfaction before he answered. 'Not a lot, Tref, although I was down by the Post Office calling my son in Banwen from the phone box and I happened to look over the wall into the yard behind the Post Office. You wouldn't believe it, but I saw that Gwilym Williams throwing sticks up at that yuge conker tree that he's got in the yard there! I mean, that's the sort of thing that kids do, but you don't 'spect to see a grown man doing it, do you?'

Trefor leaned on the bar thinking, there's more to this bit of *clecs*. So he said encouragingly, 'Go on, Dai.'

'Well, after I had finished talking to my son David, I stood and watched him for a while. He had a big basket with him and was going back and forth and around the yard collecting conkers. I thought at first he was cleaning up the yard, but that didn't make any sense to me. If you're cleaning up, why are you knocking them down to make more mess?'

Trefor smiled. 'Right enough, Dai. Why indeed?'

'So later in the day, I got curious.'

'Nothing wrong in being curious, Dai. So what did you find out, mun?'

'He's bluddy selling them, Tref! I went into the shop and there on the counter was two big baskets half filled with conkers. The little ones he was asking tuppence each for and the large ones had a price of three pence each. I thought to myself: What a bluddy man! When I was a kid and we went to throw sticks for conkers, the owners of the trees were only too glad to see us cleaning up the mess, innit?'

While this conversation was taking place, Johnny had got up from his seat to replenish his and Alan's drinks, while Colin took his place at the card game.

'Dai,' Johnny said, 'I couldn't help but overhear you saying about that Gwilym Williams and the conkers. It reminded me: when I was a young boy, me and my father were going early early over to Penderyn to see the sheepdog trials up by the Ring of Trees. I don't know if you know where that is, but it is a favourite picnic place on the Squire's land and he lets people use it. Well, this particular morning I could see some yuge conkers on the trees in the churchyard and I found a good stick and started to throw it up at these conkers. Well, my dad said, "Let me see if I can knock a few down for you." He searched around and found a big rock about the size of half a house brick. He flung this up into the tree and missed the conkers but that big stone came off a branch and bounced onto the roof of the vicarage, making 'ell of a clatter. This was about six o'clock in the morning, mind. So, we had to run like 'ell down the lane and away before anyone could see us.' He laughed, remembering that little escapade from his childhood.

Trefor stood up straight from his leaning position. 'So, Mr Councillor, you haven't always been a good boy, then!'

'Apparently not! But I have to say, kids back then had a lot more freedom and people were, shall we say, more understanding – not like today, when some people want to call the police if a kid drops a sweet wrapper on the pavement. No, things were a lot different then. Sorry, Dai – I interrupted your story. Please continue.' He picked up the two pints and made his way back to the card game.

Dai took another swig from his drink and said, 'Where was I, Tref? Oh aye! Yes, I saw those two baskets on the counter and thought, he's like that Scrooge character, trying his best to get something out of little kids for conkers, instead of giving them away. That would be a kinder thing to do, wouldn't it?'

'Yes, Dai, but it wouldn't do for everybody to be exactly the same, would it? Just pick someone in your mind that you don't think much of and then imagine everyone like that.'

Dai stared off into the distance for a moment and laughed. 'Aye, Tref. I see what you mean. I never thought of it like that before. Yes, I suppose it takes all types. Thanks.' He went across the room to sit beside Old John.

'*Bore da*, John. *Shomai?*'

'*Iawn, diolch.*' Both men spoke Welsh as their first language, but since everyone around them spoke English, it was much easier to speak that language in general conversation. When they were together, though, they spoke Welsh.

'Yes, John. I was just tellin' Trefor about that Gwilym at the Post Office trying to sell conkers to the kids. That bluddy man is a disgrace as a human being, isn't he?'

Colin, only a couple of chairs away, hearing Gwilym Williams' name, turned in his seat and asked, 'So, what's new then, Dai? I yerd you say a little bit about the Post Office.'

'That bloke down there has some baskets of conkers for sale! How mean can you get?'

'What we should do is this,' Colin said. 'A crowd of us could go in there, all askin' 'im for somethin' off the top shelf and all at the same time, and in the confusion, just walk away with the baskets. That way he would 'ave put a lot of work into somethin' he doesn't 'ave any more, and there would be so many of us in his shop he wouldn't know who to blame, if he even noticed they were missing.'

Dai and Old John broke up laughing. 'That's a bluddy good idea, Col, but I don't think that would work, for the simple reason there isn't enough room for a crowd in there and his mam is always in the shop, hovering like a... a... I don't know what, watching everybody. Nice try though!' said Dai.

Alan stood up to make his way through the scattered chairs to the bar. 'Another pint, Johnny?'

'Not for me, thanks, Al. Two is my limit on a Sunday morning, or I'll be falling asleep after I've eaten and I've got a lot of work to do today.'

'Your loss, *brawd.*'

'I know, but thanks anyway.'

Colin came up to the bar, his empty glass in hand. He looked at Alan and grinned.

Alan said, 'Aye, okay, Col. I'll get that. What will it be – best bitter?'

'Nothing less, Al, and thank you.'

'So, are you working regular now?'

'Yes, still in the Pandy. I've been working there for years now. I'm finding it harder and harder to go to work since my butty got killed there, but that's life I suppose. But there you are: danger is everywhere, isn't it?'

'Well, you could join the army – there's no war on at the moment, so it's pretty safe!' quipped Alan, with a grin.

CHAPTER 22

The Hazards of Driving a Taxi

O N HIS WAY home from a long and tedious meeting in Neath, Johnny turned off the A465 and onto the back road that took him directly to the Plough Inn. It was late in the day for him but still early to be in the pub. He parked his car and crossed the road to enter through the wide-open front door.

Trefor, resplendent in his old patched jersey, originally green but now multicoloured, looked up from serving Old John Shinkins as Johnny entered the room.

'Well, well, hello Johnny! You're a bit early today – and where's your shadow?'

Johnny gave a short laugh at Trefor's cheeky reference to his brother-in-law.

'To tell you the truth, Trefor, I have no idea, but I'm pretty sure he'll turn up yere sometime tonight. I've been in council meetings down in Neath most of this afternoon, until,' he glanced at his watch, 'about half an hour or so ago.'

'Oh! So you've been busy, then!'

Johnny pulled a face. 'Yes, you could say that. I think I'll just have a bottle of pale ale, please, Trefor. I need something to quench my thirst before I go home to have my tea.' He took a quick swig from the drink Trefor placed in front of him and sighed with satisfaction. 'The only good thing to come out of that meeting was a story told to us by a councillor from another parish down the Neath Valley. I almost wet myself when I yerd this one. It could have easily been something Fred would have got into, except that he couldn't drive a car.' He began laughing in remembrance.

'Well, go on, mun!' Trefor said. 'Don't keep it all to yourself!'

'Aye, okay. Well, this chap – Cliff called him Eddie, and coming back up yere I got to wondering if it might be Alan's brother-in-law, Eddie Hall, as he lives down that way – is a part-time driver for the taxi company where he lives. Cliff said it all depends on what shift he's working at the time in the pit. It's a handy set-up for this chap: it's something to do and he makes a few bob on the side plus any tips he might get from his fares. Anyway, Cliff said there was a big celebration dance from a college in Neath that was being held down the valley in Resolven and a crowd of people from Cliff and Eddie's village were going to be there. So the owner of the taxi company asked Eddie if he would be available to drive for him, and warned him it could be a very late night. Eddie told him that would be okay because he was on afternoon shift the following day and it wouldn't matter how late he got to bed. This suited the owner very well.

'So it was agreed Eddie would take the late taxi shift that night. His duties were simple: he was to wait outside the local pub and take passengers down the valley to the dance, drop them off and go back for more. Apparently, this went on all evening until fairly late. So, he went home for a cup of tea and a bite to eat and went back to the pub car park to pick up any phone calls to collect returning fares. Everyone that he took to the dance was given two numbers to call for their return trip – the phone in the pub and the telephone kiosk outside the village pub.

'Satisfied that everything was in place, Eddie entered the pub and sat in the bar to have conversations with some of his NCB workmates. While he was waiting, he decided to roll himself a few cigarettes from an ancient Oxo tin of loose tobacco, which no self-respecting smoker would touch with a bargepole. There was barely any tobacco in the paper and each end tapered to a point so when a match was applied, it flared up to almost nothing and the cigarette was finished.

'His first call for a return fare came at closing time in the pub, about 11 p.m. He was out of the door like a jack rabbit and on his way to Resolven. From then on, he was back and forth running a quick shuttle service. But after one trip, he turned onto the main A465 road and was about half a mile from the junction when he saw two cars collide, blocking the road. Eddie stopped his car and switched off the engine and sat for a few moments, then got out and started to walk towards the scene of the accident. Moments later, a patrolling police car coming from the direction of Glynneath passed him on the wrong side of the road. Eddie hurried towards the scene and was the first person to arrive, after the police car. The local policeman said to Eddie, "So how in the world did this happen? Did you see anything?"

'"I only saw it from a distance, but I know this chap," said Eddie, pointing to the passenger, who was lying barely moving in the passenger seat, with a cut on his forehead. The driver had climbed out of his car and was standing nearby with a dazed expression on his face. The policeman asked him if he was okay and he replied that he was.

'The policeman nodded and went on his radio to call for an ambulance and a tow company to clear the road. He called Eddie over and said, "If you know this chap and you saw something of what happened, I would like you to come with me back to the station to make a statement. Is that okay?"

'"Of course," Eddie said, "No problem!"

'The ambulance and the tow truck arrived almost at the same

time. With everything under control, for the moment anyway, Eddie followed the constable to his car and they went back to Glynneath to take his statement.

'In the meantime, Eddie's passengers in Resolven were getting concerned that there was no sign of him arriving to take them home. Eventually one of the girls, who lived next door to the owner of the taxi company, called his house and got him out of bed, which didn't sit too well with him. Irritated, he jumped in his car and went to look for Eddie.

'By this time, Tref,' went on Johnny, 'the blockage to the A465 had been cleared and there was no sign of the crash, but there was Eddie's taxi parked at the side of the road with no sign of its driver. His boss turned around and went back to the village to get a spare set of keys and took a spare driver with him. He got in Eddie's taxi and went down the valley to Resolven to collect the stranded passengers. Him and his spare driver between them ran a shuttle service until all their customers were safely home.

'In the meantime, the Glynneath constable drove Eddie back to where he had left his taxi, and discovered it had gone. So, naturally Eddie had to report it stolen. 'So what happened next, Trefor, is hilarious! He was taken home in the police car. A few minutes after that Eddie saw his taxi parked just up the road from his house. He thought some local youngster had taken his taxi for a ride home. He jumped in it and decided to continue his job of bringing his fares from Resolven.

'It so happened there was a police patrol car coming down the valley, and they spotted Eddie driving in the opposite direction. They turned around and chased after him, blue lights flashing. He saw this coming up behind and pulled over to let them pass. Not a chance. They stopped right behind him and arrested him for driving a stolen vehicle. He told them he was the official driver of the car and that he'd been a witness to a crash earlier and had been to make a statement with the constable in Glynneath. They thought this was a likely story, so they said, "We'll pop up to Glynneath to verify your story, okay?" He said, "What about my car, then?" but was told, "Leave it where it is!"

'Of course, he replied, "*Bois bach!* I've got paying passengers to bring home from Resolven – they're depending on me!"

'Apparently, the policemen looked at each other as if doubting their own judgment, then said, "Sorry, mate. Get in the patrol car please."

Arriving at Glynneath Police Station, Eddie went in front of them into the office and the constable looked up in surprise from his volumes of paperwork. "What are you doing back yere again, Eddie?"

'The two patrolmen looked a bit embarrassed as Eddie turned and said, "See! I told you the truth."

'When the sequence of events was explained in detail, they all had a good laugh, but it wasn't explained so easily to the owner of the taxis! He'd been dragged out of bed at 1.30 in the morning and had had to find another driver after seeing his empty taxi on the main road and then having to drive the taxi himself to pick up customers; all this, while he didn't have a clue where Eddie had disappeared to!

'Apparently, he told Eddie that he'd thought about sacking him for all the potch he had to go though to bring his customers back home, but he grudgingly found it funny in the end.

'Well, boys. When I heard that in Neath this afternoon, I laughed so much the tears ran down my 'legs'

As he finished the story, Old John and Trefor broke up laughing with him.

'Oh *Duw*! Wait until I pass that one on later tonight. I'm sure some of the boys yere will know who he is – p'raps they worked with him.'

'Aye! You never know. It's a fairly close community around

yere, innit? Especially among the colliers. And I'll ask Alan in case it is his brother-in-law.'

Later that evening, as Trefor related Johnny's hilarious story, Danny Thomas said, 'Aye, I know him. What a bluddy character he is. He was up in court last year for poaching a salmon from the Nedd. A water bailiff came up behind him in the dark and caught him lifting this big fish out of the water. He took the fish off him and said he would be charged with poaching. He tried to take Eddie's rod and tackle off him but Eddie was a lot bigger than him and held his rod away from him. He asked Eddie for his name and address but he wouldn't give it so the bailiff followed him back to his car and took his registration number, and that's how he got the summons in the post. Eddie thought that was a bit of a laugh, because he himself is a water bailiff for a club over in the Rhondda.

'Anyway, he appeared in court in Neath and the story I yerd was this. When the charge of poaching a salmon from the Nedd was read out in court, Eddie was asked how he wanted to plead. He said, "Not guilty. I am pleading not guilty, sir."

'Then he was asked who was in the court to represent him.

'He stood up and said, "Nobody. I will speak for myself, sir."

'So the water bailiff was there and gave his version of the incident, and said he observed the defendant illegally taking the salmon from the river and that he had brought the fish as evidence to court to prove it.

'It was then Eddie sprang a surprise on everyone. He stood up and said in a loud voice, "That is not a salmon, Judge. It is what we call in Wales a sewin or sea trout, and it is not illegal to take them from that river. I know this because I am a water bailiff in another district, sir."

'This water bailiff jumped up. "It is a salmon I have yere," he said, pointing to the large fish on the table.

'Eddie laughed at him and said, "All you have to do is count the scales behind the gills. If there are seven scales it's a sewin. Go on, count them!" Moments later the water bailiff, red-faced, stood up again and said, "I'm sorry sir, but I'm afraid he's right."

'According to this chap in work, Eddie had told him there would be no problem and he would get off with the charge of poaching against him and he went to court just to see. He said the court was in an uproar with some people cheering for Eddie. Of course, he was all smiles when the judge dismissed the case against him. As I said before, this Eddie is 'ell of a boy and a real character.'

CHAPTER 23

The Secret to Catching Trout

A T 3 A.M. the butcher picked up his phone. Moments later Trefor, who had been dozing in his armchair near the open door of his Aga range, awoke with a start. Automatically he stood up to go and unplug the phone, glancing up at the clock on the wall above him.

'Damn it all! It's that bluddy butcher again,' he muttered to himself, 'He should be asleep like normal people at this time of the morning!' He sighed, walked across the kitchen and unplugged his phone from the socket in the wall. He settled back down in the comfort of his armchair to sleep until morning, secure in the knowledge that the butcher would be getting more annoyed by the second when his phone call could not be connected.

The following evening when Johnny and Alan came into the bar, it was the last thing on Trefor's mind to tell them about the butcher's continued telephone call nonsense. He saw them come in, but his mind was elsewhere, thinking of ways to repay and perhaps embarrass the butcher again.

Hmmm,' he thought, the Post Office Telephone people called me last week to ask if I would be interested in exchanging my old phone for one of the new-style models. They said I could have it installed right alongside my own phone with a separate line and a different number to try it for a few weeks. Yes, and if I liked it, they would be prepared to change it free of charge. Now that has a nice ring to it, 'free of charge'. Now there's a thought, boys.

'Huh? What was that, Alan? Oh, two pints is it?'

Johnny nudged Alan. 'Hey, Al! Look at our landlord, will you? I can sense he is planning another little surprise for someone.'

Alan grinned as he asked. 'Are you sure, Johnny?'

'Oh yes. I haven't been in this man's company all these years, without being able to see when he's plotting something. He leaves little pointers so you can easily tell. Look at his eyes, Al! You can almost see the wheels turning.'

Trefor smiled as he placed the two pints on the bar in front of them. Johnny picked up his pint and took a small sip of the milk-like foam. 'C'mon, Tref! Spit it out. What are you up to now, then?'

Trefor beamed, then said. 'Not a thing, Johnny. Not a single thing and that's the truth, boys.'

Johnny stepped back a pace from the bar as he closely eyed Trefor's smiling features. 'My instincts haven't let me down before, have they, Al?'

Alan grinned. 'Not that I know of, *brawd*!'

Trefor shrugged as if he didn't care what they thought and turned away to serve Danny Thomas, who had just come up to the bar in time to hear some of their conversation.

'Yes, sir! What'll it be – a pint of best bitter?'

'Nah! I think I'll just have a bottle of light ale to liven up my pint over there.' He nodded in the direction of the large card table. 'I've let it stand for too long, chopsin' about the best places around yere for trout. I thought I knew all the little tricks for catching them but this one was a new one on me. Remember the other day, there was a story going around about some clown called Eddie Hall and his antics with the police and an arrest for stealing a taxi down in the Neath valley…?'

'Aye, aye, Danny!' Johnny interrupted, with a laugh. 'It was me who brought that story back yere and we all had a good laugh about it. He's Alan's brother-in-law and he's not a clown, by the way, it's just that things happen to him without him trying. It's amazing really. Sorry for the interruption Danny – please, go on with your story.'

Danny took a swig from the neck of the bottle. 'Well, it seems some of the members of the Rhondda Angling Club had got together up at Llyn Fawr for a bit of a competition amongst themselves.' He nodded in the general direction of the large lake/reservoir below the mountain called Craig y Llyn. 'Well, this same Eddie bloke was up there too, with his fly rod. I was told he's a member of the same angling club and is a water bailiff for them too. Anyway, the story is, they'd been fishing as a group for a few hours and hadn't had a bite or even a sniff of any fish at all. Now, this was pretty unusual, because a few of them had won cups in competitions all over the place for fly fishing. Along comes this Eddie bloke and he stops to have a chat for a while, then he walks away from them and sits on the bank just about a hundred or so feet from them – and within a few minutes he was pulling trout after trout out of the water in front of them. So a couple of the boys went over to see what he was using for bait. Would you believe it if I told you he was using bread and Marmite! And when he had caught his limit, he picked up his tackle and walked away down the mountain back to his village, Well, those boys from the Rhondda were gobsmacked.'

'No!' said Trefor laughing. 'I don't know a thing about fishing but that sounds an absolutely hilarious way to catch fish. Is it legal to do that?'

'I don't know about being legal but it was enough to get the other anglers up there really annoyed, that one of their own could pull a stunt like that and right under their noses too. He's a cheeky sod mind, innit? I yerd after what he'd done. He got some thick slices of bread and plastered it with Marmite, then he rolled it up into pellets and had them in the pockets of his coat and as he walked along he was flinging a few of them into the water and the bluddy fish followed the trail right to where he was sitting and they jumped onto his hook to be pulled kicking and screaming from the water. What a dirty trick to play on his own club members, though.'

They all started laughing at the image Danny had described in such detail for them.

Johnny, his eyes full of mischief, said without smile on his face, 'I think I might have a story something like that about the way to catch a trout. It will have you in fits, boys, but it is not a story that would have been written down by Izaak Walton, mind.'

Danny looked at Johnny with some suspicion. 'Who's this Izaak bloke when he's at home, then?'

'Oh, he wrote a book about fishing called *The Compleat Angler*, donkey's years ago, and my story has nothing to do with him, okay? To catch a trout: first you have to find a nice little stream with good clear water.' Trefor, Danny and Alan gathered closer as Johnny lowered his voice. 'Then you place a good clean house brick in the water. Next you get some white pepper and plaster a fresh piece of lettuce with it and put it on top of the brick and weigh it down with a small stone. The trap is now set! Now, the trout is a curious creature and it will go up to the lettuce to see what it is. When it sniffs the pepper, it will make it sneeze and it will knock itself out on the brick. All you have to do then is pick it up and take it home.' Each of them, open mouthed, looked at each other, wondering what was coming next, but Johnny, straight-faced, picked up his pint and took a long swig.

There was complete silence for a split second, then they all roared with laughter. Danny, holding onto the bar with one hand for support as the tears ran down his cheeks, gave Johnny a push as he said weakly, 'Get away from yere, you bluddy *twpsyn*! And we all fell for that one, boys! Like a bunch of idiots!'

Alan just stood there shaking his head as he looked at his brother-in-law. 'Honestly Tref, I don't know where he gets some of these stories from. Some of them are like tea from China!' Seeing the puzzled look on Trefor's round features, he added. 'Pretty far-fetched, Tref!'

Danny walked away, shaking his head in disbelief at the fairy tale he had just listened to from Johnny.

'How about that one, Tref?' Johnny said, smiling broadly. 'That's one for the books, innit?'

'Oh, aye!' Trefor replied, grinning. 'Yes, that's one for the books, all right!'

He glanced up at the big clock on the wall behind him and saw it was coming up to closing time. He raised his voice. 'Hey, boys! I will be closing right on time tonight! We've got a new policeman in the village and I'm told he's pretty keen, so get ready to drink up when I call time. I don't want another day in court, thank you very much, okay?'

In his normal voice he said, 'Yes, Dai Bandit's nickname for this chap is Bookum! He knows him from where he used to live down by Neath and he said what he's like. I'm told he's got one of those new generation of silent motorbikes, whatever they are.'

'Yes,' Johnny said. 'I've seen him out and about on it. It's a called a Velocette and it has an aluminium fairing. You can't hear the damn thing running, hardly!'

Alan pulled a face at Johnny's technical description for this new motorbike.

'I have to say, though, it looks miles too small for that lengthy cop. He must be 6 foot 5 at least, don't you think?'

Trefor smiled. 'Well, he is very tall. I got a stiff neck just looking up at him this morning.'

'Yes, he is. I was talking to Barney over by the New Inn the other day after someone had broken into his little Morris car...'

Trefor held up a hand. 'Who's this Barney, then, Alan?'

'Oh, he's a chap I know from Waun-gron. He lives next door but one to the New Inn. Anyway, he was telling me that when Bookum showed up, he brought his fingerprint kit with him and what a mess he made of that little exercise. Barney said his car looked like it had been in a dust storm. That white powder was everywhere, and if he had a tidy suit on, this stuff would stick to his clothes. He said it took bluddy days to get his car clean – and after all that, they never caught anyone. He said that the only other thing to come out of that day was that he got charged for having his tax disc out of date by about two years. When Bookum told him off about it, he said he didn't know because he left all that stuff to his wife and he was going to give her a good telling off too, after.

'Although Barney did say this: Bookum told him he really loves his job, especially when he knows that the people he's charged with an offence would be pleading guilty when they appeared in court.'

'That's as maybe, Alan, but some of the policemen when I was growing up in this village would take some beating!' said Johnny. 'They didn't have fancy motorbikes or cars to get around the parish. In their day, they walked the beat everywhere and in whatever the weather threw at them, and were always pretty fair in dealing with everyone.'

At that moment, old Tommy James came up to the bar just in time to hear the tail-end of their conversation.

'Talking about policemen in the old days, eh? I can tell you a few stories about coppers from when I was living over in Blaengwynfi. Der! One of the blokes in the village was a part-time gravedigger and he had this job to do one night in the local cemetery, and this place had a reputation for being haunted.

Well, he'd been digging for quite a few hours so he climbed out of the grave to have a spell, like. Well, he looked over the wall and saw the local policeman coming towards him in the dark and he called out to ask him the time. At the inquest, he said the policeman grabbed his chest and dropped dead right in front of him!'

Tommy James picked up his pint and without a backward glance, made his way across the room to his seat at the large kitchen card table, leaving Trefor and the two councillors open-mouthed at the bar.

CHAPTER 24

Barney and the Home Brew

JOHNNY AND ALAN were chatting to Trefor in their usual spot at the far end of the bar in the Plough when Johnny turned to Trefor and said, 'Did I ever tell you about my adventures in making home-brew beer?'

'What?!' Alan exclaimed, laughing. 'You're admitting to making beer in open competition with Trefor yere's best bitter? Shame on you, Johnny.'

'No, no, of course not! I just did it to see if it could be a bit of a hobby, that's all.'

'Well, I hope you're not expecting to take any of my customers, Johnny. I'm barely making a living as it is, with that Gwilym the Post and his bluddy off-licence.'

'No, no, Tref, this was for personal consumption only. It was the first time I tried to make this Yorkshire bitter ale. I was in Aberdare and I saw this home-brew mix advertised in one of the shops. It had all the instructions and looked easy enough to make. One of the bits in the box was a large plastic bag. In this you mixed all the ingredients. This was the substitute for a barrel and when you'd mixed everything together, you needed to keep it at an even temperature while it fermented. What a bluddy laugh that was. I put it on a shelf in our airing cupboard in our upstairs bathroom. Our house smelt like brewery fr'ages. My wife said it reminded her of going past Evan Evans Bevan's brewery on the bus into Neath. I had to give this bag a bit of a shake every day before I went to work and I suppose the build-up of gas leaked out of the top where I had tied it together – damn, it was strong!'

'Aye, aye!' Alan chipped in, laughing. 'I remember opening your back door and the pong hit you in the face. Your missus was right enough, Johnny – it did smell like a bluddy brewery. Anyway, go on.'

Trefor came back to join them. 'What smelt like a brewery?'

'Oh, Johnny's house with his home brew.'

'Aye, aye, Tref, fair play: it did. I don't know how she puts up with some of my nonsense at times. Anyway, to get back to my story. After all this had finished brewing, I got a load of flagon bottles and one very large Long Tom whiskey bottle – it was yuge. It took me ages to filter this beer into the bottle cos you had to be careful not to get any of the bits from the bottom of the bag into the flagons. Anyway, I got this done and pushed brand new corks into them.

'Now comes the funny part. The instructions said to keep them all at an even temperature for about a week or perhaps a bit more. So, I decided to stand them all around the hearth and I put the yuge bottle to one side of the fireplace. We had a big fireguard, and after dinner I would sit in front of the fire in a big swivel rocking chair with my feet up on the guard. Well, on this particular evening I was dozing in my chair when all of a sudden there was this tremendous bang. I shot backwards off my chair onto the floor. At first, I thought some kid had thrown a stone at our window. I pulled back the curtains, but the street was empty. It turned out it was the cork out of the whiskey bottle that had shot off around the room, and some of the other corks in the flagons did the same too. Later, when I tried the brew, it tasted even stronger than a bottle of IPA.'

'Get away,' Trefor laughed. 'How in the world can a home brew be stronger than a professionally made beer? Pint is it?' He turned away to pull a pint for Old John Shinkins.

'Go on Johnny, I'm listening.' Old John, being a bit curious about their laughter, stood nearby, sipping his fresh pint.

Johnny nodded in his direction and replied. 'Okay, Tref, here's why my home brew was stronger. In the last stage, before you bottle it, the instructions said to put a small amount of sugar in there before the beer goes in. Well, I put about double the amount recommended, just in case.'

'Well, that was a bit daft,' Alan said.

'No, it was better than putting too little, innit?'

Everybody broke up laughing and Old John chipped in. 'I can remember my old granny making what she called "small beer", and that was bluddy strong too. I remember as a little boy taking a bottle to have a swig of it. Boys, I didn't know where I was and that's the truth.'

'And you haven't stopped drinking since,' said Alan, laughing out loud at the expression on Old John's face.

'No, I haven't, now I come to think of it, Alan.' Old John grinned and they watched him make his way slowly back to his favourite seat on the wooden settle beside the stove.

'To get back to my story, boys,' continued Johnny, 'I was in the New Inn one night...'

Trefor looked at him, eyebrows raised.

Johnny grinned. 'I was in there just for one pint, Trefor. I'd promised to meet someone there, that's all.'

Trefor shrugged, grinning as he polished a pint glass, holding it up to the light and looking for the slightest blemish.

'Well anyway, who should be there in the men's bar but Barney, and Alan knows how he can drink. Eight or ten pints, p'raps more if he's on form. He and a few others were talking about home brew and how it compared to best bitter in strength. I just couldn't resist telling Barney I'd made some home brew which could knock the socks off any best bitter around. It was a bit of an exaggeration, mind, but I thought it might shut them up. That didn't work for a minute because Barney said he didn't believe a word of it and I, like a *twpsyn*, took it as a bit of a challenge. I told him I'd bring him a flagon for him to try next time I was passing his house. Anyway, a couple of nights later, I brought one of them with me and let myself in – he never locks his door – and left it on his kitchen table, then called in the New Inn to let him know it was there.

'Well, a few nights later I went back to the New Inn to meet this chap and Dai Bricks caught my arm as I went in. "Hey," he said, "what the 'ell did you put in that flagon of home brew you gave to Barney the other night?" I was laughing when I asked him why. "Well," he said, "you know I travel to and from work with Barney because I don't drive. Well, the morning after you left him that flagon of home brew, I was ready and waiting to go to work but there was no sign of Barney coming for me. So in the end I walked over to his place and it was all in darkness. I went in and shouted for him but I got no reply. I went upstairs and found him still in bed, fast asleep. I shouted at him and had to give him a bit of a shake to wake him up. He looked like he didn't know where he was or even what day it was. After, he told me he'd drunk your flagon when he got home after a few in the New Inn, and that's the last thing he remembered. Yere's the funny part though. When he got up from his bed and went to put on one of those high boots he wears, he found it was full to the brim with pee – and not a drop anywhere on the floor, so drunk as he was, his aim must have been pretty good."

'I had a good laugh with Dai over that, but Barney has never said one word about it. P'raps I should remind him one day.'

Alan laughing, clapped his brother-in-law on the shoulder.

Trefor said. 'That was a good one, Johnny. Have you made any more since?'

'No, Tref: once was enough, thank you. Two pints please.'

Roy, standing at the bar, said. 'There's a lot of laughter coming from this corner – what's going on, then?'

'A pint of best, is it, Roy?' Trefor, smiling broadly, turned and asked him.

'Yes, Tref, and a small bottle of Guinness, please. You didn't answer me.'

'Oh, Johnny was relating a story about Barney from over by the New Inn, peeing in his boot after drinking a flagon of Johnny's home brew.'

Alan turned towards Roy. 'And I yerd a story a long time ago when you had a bit of a problem having a pee, Roy.'

'Aye, I did and I don't want reminding of that either. It was a bit embarrassing.'

'Oh? Well, go on, Roy,' said Trefor, placing the foaming pint in front of him.

Looking a bit sheepish, Roy said, 'I'd been drinking in yere, Tref, and we'd had a pretty good night. I got home all right and went to bed. In the middle of the night I got up, busting for a pee, and knew I wouldn't make it downstairs to the toilet. Our house has those very wide window sills and it being in the middle of the night, I thought: it won't harm if I take a pee from the window. So I was standing on the window sill, enjoying myself, when a light flashed on me. I looked down and there was our local copper, asking me what I thought I was doing. So, I told him I was having a pee. He said, "I can see that, but wouldn't it be better if you opened the bottom part of the window and not the top?"

I looked down and yes, he was right enough. The bluddy window and my feet were soaking wet.'

They all broke up laughing, staggering around holding their sides as if in pain.

Later, when things had calmed down a bit, Alan leaned back against the bar to survey the crowded, smoke-filled room. 'There's a good crowd of boys coming yere, isn't there, Johnny?'

'Aye, you're right! Couldn't wish for better. There you are. We're all from yere, grew up together and worked together – well, most of them – and for a small village, we've done pretty well. How many full Internationals do you think came from yere?'

'I dunno... but off the top of my head I can safely say two: Dai Morris and Glyn Shaw in rugby.'

'Right! I think there are a couple more but I can't remember them right away... but I will remember, if I have enough time.'

'Talking of time, it's time for me to go home and get some sleep – I'm on the early shift in the morning. So, I'll see you tomorrow, *brawd*.' Alan raised his hand to Johnny, Trefor and the crowd as he left the Plough.

CHAPTER 25

Barney gets a Fright

IT WAS SUNDAY morning and the main bar in the Plough Inn was crowded with the usual suspects having their pre-lunch pint. The door into the main bar opened and Will 'Snuffy' Price came in, his features alive with excitement. He paused for a moment, eyeing the crowd around the big table, where the inevitable game of four-handed crib was taking place. Then, as if making up his mind, he turned away and made his way to the bar.

Trefor looked up from pulling a pint for Willi Bray. 'Oh, hello, Snuffy, what are you doing in yere on a Sunday morning?'

Snuffy Price was a short, tubby little man and with his cap on, he was less than half an inch taller than Willi Bray. He didn't live in Rhyd-y-groes but he had worked for many years with most of Trefor's customers in the local coal mines. He got his nickname, Snuffy, from his frequent use of tobacco snuff, which not only stained his bushy moustache a dark brown but also the back of his left hand and the front of his shirt and waistcoat.

'Der, Trefor!' he said in a loud voice, attracting the attention of others waiting to be served at the bar. 'I've just come from the New Inn. Aye, I was in the men's bar having a quiet pint and watching some of the boys over there playing Nap...'

'What in the world is Nap, Snuffy? I don't think I've ever yerd of that game,' Trefor looked at him, a bit puzzled.

'Oh, that's short for Napoleon. It's a card game and the boys over there play it for money. There's usually five players and they each put a shilling into the pool and they are dealt five cards. Each player has the chance to bid on how many tricks they can win to take the pool. Anyway, this morning, as I said, I was standing by the bar having a pint when that chap Barney, I think he works in that colliery in Cwmgwrach, was having a game of Nap with an Irish chap from Glynneath and three other chaps I don't know…'

'Where are you going with this story, Snuffy?" Trefor rolled his eyes up to the ceiling.

'Oh aye! Just a minute, Tref – I'm coming to it. Anyway, Barney kept on outbidding this Irish chap to save the pool until he had a decent chance to win it himself and scoop the pool. Well, he did this a few times while I was watching, and this Irish chap told him, "Barney, if you do that to me again, I'll bluddy kill you and that's a fact! I'm tellin' you now for the last time!"

'Well, Barney just laughed and shrugged his shoulders. The thing is, boys, Barney probably had rubbish in his hand because after he played his first card, he grabbed the pack of cards and mixed his into them without anyone knowing if he could have won the pool. That's like cheating to me.

'This morning though, when he'd just outbid this Irish chap, Mike, for the third time, Mike stood up and said, "That's it Barney! I've already warned you!" With that, he pulled a gun from his inside pocket and fired two shots right at Barney's chest. Well, boys, there was a place!'

'What?!' Trefor raised his voice, looking at the shocked faces all around the bar. 'He shot Barney in front of everyone?'

'Aye, he did. It turned out after it was a bluddy cap gun, but it looked so real. What a noise it made, and smoke everywhere.

Barney fell back against the seat holding his chest and shouting for the police and a doctor at the same time. Mrs Lewis ran into the bar shouting at the top of her voice for this Irish chap to get out, but he was rolling around, laughing fit to bust and waving the toy gun in the air and shouting, "I got you this time, Barney!" The gun looked real enough, mind, chrome-plated with black grip handles. Everyone in the bar looked shocked, including me, until we could see it was a toy gun.

'I'm telling you now, boys, it frightened the bluddy life out of Barney. P'raps he won't be so quick in future to cheat and rob the pool.

'Mrs Lewis was off top – she even came around into the bar to see the gun for herself. Charlie, her husband, the landlord, just stood there grinning like the Cheshire Cat. P'raps he knew something, cos he's well aware of Barney's little tricks, and he said, "Serve you right, Barney. Time somebody put a stop to your nonsense."

'Mrs Lewis grabbed the toy gun off this Irish chap and waved it around then gave it back to him, at the same time telling him, "I don't want any more of this nonsense or I'll ban you from coming yere altogether. Are you listening to me?" I could see he was trying not to laugh.

'Then he said, "I promise, Mrs Lewis, not to shoot Barney again," then he broke up laughing again and everyone in the bar joined in, even Mrs Lewis.

'While this was going on, Barney was lying back against the seat still holding his chest. Then after it had all calmed down, Mrs Lewis told Barney that since he was the cause of it all, he'd better watch his step, or he could be banned for cheating at cards. It shocked him into silence and the rest of us into laughing at the comical expression on his face. Thinking back, this Irish chap must have put in double caps in that gun because it was so loud in that small room and all the bluddy smoke from it, innit?'

'Well, *bois bach*!' Trefor turned to everyone who was listening to Snuffy's story. 'I'll have to watch out for this mad Irishman, won't I?'

'I don't think so, Tref. I know him pretty well and Mike only comes up to the New Inn on a Sunday morning for a game of cards. There always a little bit of money on the games over there. It's nothing to worry about,' said Twm.

'Oh, that's all right then – I'll take your word for it, Twm.' Trefor turned to serve the others waiting patiently at the bar.

Twm, sipping his beer as he walked slowly back to his seat at the card table, sat down heavily and said, 'You all yerd about that Barney in the New Inn, boys! That bluddy man 'ave done that to me a few times and I told 'im to pack it in, but he don't listen, do he?'

'I wouldn't play cards with 'im, Twm,' Bobby said picking up the deck of cards.

'Right enough,' Twm replied. 'P'raps the boys over there will watch 'im from now on.'

'It's not often that a leopard will change his spots, mind,' Alan was grinning as he said it. 'It's the way Barney plays. You just have to play him at his own game. I've played cards with him and others a lot and I always know when he has a good hand. He will move back in his seat in case somebody – in fact anybody not even playing – sees any of his cards, then he will look at each player in turn. I know this cos I've watched him any amount of times doing it. So, there you are boys, Barney's secret is out. What I do when I play cards with him, I bid in front of him if I think he's got a good hand, right!'

'Oh, aye! So that's why you always sit on his right, is it?' Johnny laughed.

Alan didn't reply, just grinned and said. 'Okay, boys, enough about Barney – let's play cards.'

Chapter 26

Adventures in DIY

'**Y**OU, DIPSTICK! YOU bluddy dipstick! There is no other word to describe what you and your nonsense have caused in yere today, Eddie Hall!'

To say that Marion was a little bit upset would have been something of a major understatement.

It was early summer and Alan, her husband, had recently been promoted to site foreman on the local opencast operation. The job entailed so much paperwork and administration that it seemed he had little time for anything else at the end of a twelve-hour shift, seven days a week, and several months after them moving to Cwmgwrach, various DIY jobs still needed doing. It had seemed quite fortunate at the time that Eddie, her sister's husband, worked on much easier shifts, and had some free time to do odd jobs. You could also say it was fate when she happened to mention that she had a few 'little jobs' that needed doing around the house, and he immediately generously volunteered his services to do them.

She had a few doubts but, with the high cost of getting the services of a tradesman to do the job, she eventually decided to accept his offer.

His first 'little job' was to change the hot water boiler in the lean-to conservatory adjoining the kitchen. It was all going well until he tried to disconnect the boiler from the water main without first thinking too much about the pressure connection. Consequently, when he loosened the connection, the incoming pressure blew it out of his hand and flooded the two downstairs rooms. Drenched to the skin, he managed to turn off the rushing water at the mains supply outside the back door. In doing that, he completely forgot about the water already in the boiler, which, left unattended, continued to leak heavily while he was busy with a mop sweeping the first flood out through the open back door.

This calamitous situation resulted in Marion contacting a local plumber on his after-hours emergency number, in order to rectify the devastation Eddie had created, and thus cost her a lot of money into the bargain.

Two weeks later, after all recriminations had been dealt with in the family and peace reigned once more, he was, for all his faults, once again back in her good books. It was then she mentioned that there was a tiled fireplace in her upstairs bedroom that she wanted to get rid of.

'Funny you should say that!' he said. 'I've been looking for one of them to put in my front room cos the old one has got a crack in it. I'll take it out for you, if you like! I'll even buy it off you!'

She looked at him for a few moments speculatively and then, against her better judgement, Marion allowed her forgiving and generous nature to overrule her natural instinct and she agreed he could have the job of removing the fireplace and then take it at no cost.

He arrived mid morning the following day armed with a bag of tools, and began removing the tiles surrounding the fireplace. By teatime he had the fireplace out in one piece and had laid it flat on the carpet in front of the double bed. Then, for some reason known only to himself, he removed a large section of the floorboards and then inexplicably pulled the carpet back in place over the open area.

Meanwhile, the lady of the house was busy, immediately below, in the kitchen, preparing a roast dinner for her husband's return from work. Just before he was due home, she decided to go upstairs, dreading the mess she might find, while Eddie was outside having a smoke. She stood for a few moments just inside the door as she surveyed the room, then decided to take a closer look at what he had been doing. She walked towards the open gap in the wall and suddenly she went down through the hole in the floorboards and sat abruptly on the carpet, her legs dangling through the downstairs kitchen ceiling. Then, just as suddenly, her weight hitting the bedroom floor somehow dislodged many years of soot, which descended on her like a shower of rain through the gap where the fireplace had been, covering her and going through the open floor into the kitchen below and all over the plates of dinner she had placed on the table. She coughed and spluttered as she screamed Eddie's name at the top of her voice.

Her screams of fright and anger brought Eddie running flat out through the total devastation in the kitchen and up the stairs to where Marion was still shouting his name.

He stopped dead in his tracks and almost laughed at the sight of her sitting on the carpeted floor with her face as black as a moonless night and everywhere around her covered in soot.

'Get me out of yere, you bluddy dipstick,' she demanded in a tight voice, gritting her teeth in anger. 'What the 'ell have you done this time, Eddie?'

He leaned over her and caught hold of her arm but found he was unable to move her. 'Listen, I've got to get some help. I'll be back in minute, okay?'

Before she could say anything, she could hear him clattering down the stairs. It was as much as she could do not to scream out loud when she found she was unable to turn around to see what devastation that was behind her. There was a thick covering of soot over everything she could see. It was all across the pure white linen sheets that she had recently laid out in preparation for changing the bed... although she only had to look down at herself to imagine what the rest of the room must look like. At that moment, she heard the sound of her husband's noisy diesel work vehicle coming to a stop outside.

Seconds later her husband, with Eddie in tow, appeared beside her. Unspeaking, they each grabbed an arm and carefully lifted her as gently as possible out of the gaping hole in the floor.

Once on her feet, she spun around to face Eddie, her fists clenched. 'Get away from me before I give you a biff, you, you, you – I don't know what to call you!'

Eddie, shamefaced, started to leave the room, then turned back suddenly and asked, 'Er, what about my fireplace, then?'

She looked at him, her mouth open in shock. 'Fireplace?' she shouted at the top of her voice. She took a step towards him. 'FIREPLACE? I'll give you bluddy fireplace!'

Her husband, doing his best to keep a straight face, looked at her, covered in soot with only the whites of her eyes visible. He just pointed to the bedroom door and Eddie disappeared.

Alan reached out and drew her into his arms as she began to sob in anger and frustration. She leaned heavily against his chest, all the while muttering. 'I should have known better! I should have known better from before. Just look at this mess, will you!'

He said softly. 'Never mind the mess up yere. Wait till you see the mess he's made in the kitchen. First things first though. Are *you* okay? Apart from you looking like someone ready to audition for a part in a minstrel show!'

She looked at him in silence for a few moments, doing her best not to laugh at the image her mind projected. Suddenly, they both broke into hysterical laughter, which broke the tension they had both felt.

Downstairs was like a disaster zone, with layers of soot covering everything in sight. The plates of roast dinner she had so carefully prepared and laid out were covered in soot and she threw them into the dustbin without another thought.

'Well, so much for my roast beef dinner! It looked good though,' said Alan. 'I think the best thing you can do now is have a bath and a change of clothes, while I go out and find us some fish and chips, is it? In the meantime, don't let that bluddy terrorist back in yere, right? In the morning, I'll get one of the boys from work to give me a hand to get that fireplace down and put it out the back somewhere, okay?'

Reluctantly, she nodded agreement, lumps of soot falling from her hair and bursting into dust as they hit the floor at her soot-covered feet. She forced herself to smile as she said, 'You know, he's not such a bad bloke, it's just that he is a disaster every time he volunteers to help. Can you imagine if...'

She looked over her shoulder, but Alan had already left to go in search of their fish-and-chip supper.

CHAPTER 27

It's All in a Name

JANE WILLS TOOK a last look around the neat living room as she buttoned her coat and picked up her handbag off the coffee table.

'Yes, I'm ready! I'll be with you now, in a minute!' she called out, in reply to her husband Johnny's impatient question.

It was eight in the morning on Saturday: their usual time to leave from their house in Rhyd-y-Groes for their weekly visit to her mother in Waun-gron. It was a tedious drive down the lane to where she lived, flanked on each side by row after row of parked cars. Eventually, they arrived at her mother's house – only to find her mother and Aunty Gwen, her mother's older sister, in the midst of departure to destinations unknown, with their suitcases packed and ready to go by the front door.

Jane and Johnny looked from the two suitcases to her mother's smiling face and back again to the cases.

'So where are you two off to, then?' Johhny asked.

In unison, the two sisters replied, 'We're off to Morecambe Bay for a week by the sea!'

'Morecambe Bay! Well, you never said when we were yere last week, did you?' said Jane, in surprise.

'Well, no, *bach*! It was a spur of the moment thing,' said her mother. 'See, we were talking with Maggie Williams. She's an old friend from when we were children together in school. She lives next door but one to the Prince of Wales in Harris Street. You must remember where that is, don't you?'

Jane nodded, knowing the street well.

'Well, she runs trips all over the place. We were talking to her in the Co-op down by Merthyr Road and she told us that this coming week is pensioners' week up there and all the hotels are knocking 30% off. So me and Aunty Gwen thought it would be a good idea to take advantage of the discount and go up there for a week. She told us there was a busload going up there from the chapel. She said she was sorry there was no room on the bus, but there was plenty of room at the hotel. So we asked her to book us into the hotel with everybody else and we'll make our own way up there. All the people we know will be there and we can have a bit of fun doing those little skits we always do. You know, "The Laughing Policeman", "Three Little Maids" from Gilbert and Sullivan and that other one, "Nobody Loves a Fairy When She's Forty". It'll be a lot of fun.'

Jane and Johnny exchanged glances. Jane said, 'So what time is the bus picking you up, then?'

'Oh, there's no room on the coach for us, cariad. We were going to catch the Red and White bus to Cardiff and get a coach from there up to Morecambe Bay.'

'Well, it sounds like fun. What hotel are you staying at, then?'

'Oh, don't worry about that, Jane. Maggie Williams has booked it all for us and I've got it written down. We just have to pay her at the hotel when we get there. She told us it's the same place we stayed last Easter.'

Johnny turned towards his wife and took in a deep breath. 'Listen, Jane and me are at a bit of a loose end for the next couple of days, as I've got Monday off. So why don't we drive you up to Morecambe Bay in my new car and we can stay a couple of days, and then you can come back by train to Cardiff. You can phone us to let us know when you'll be arriving and we'll meet you and take you home to Waun-Gron.' He smiled and said, 'How does that sound?' He paused and asked, 'You haven't bought any coach tickets yet, have you?'

'No, *bach*. We were going to do that in Cardiff.'

'Well, that's good. Right! As I said, we'll take you both up to Morecambe Bay. It will do my new car the world of good to have a run like that. And you can both have a comfortable trip instead of carrying your suitcases up and down the steps on those old coaches. Right, so that's settled, then! We'll go with you, Mam!'

'Well, there's lovely, innit? Okay, then, we're in your hands, Johnny, and ready to go.' She gave Jane a brief hug and picked up her suitcase. Together they all trooped outside and put their cases in the boot of Johnny's shiny new Rover 100 car.

His mother-in-law turned back to the house to make sure the front door was locked then climbed into the back seat to sink into the soft leather seat beside her sister.

Johnny and Jane, laughing at the surprised expression on their faces, closed the doors and Jane remarked, 'Well, this is a lovely unexpected trip for us, so let's get going, is it?'

Johnny turned the car towards Penderyn Road and, after a quick detour to their own house to pack a few essentials, followed the road across the Brecon Beacons. In no time at all, they were in the market town of Brecon and turning towards Hay-on-Wye, which was followed by Leominster and Shrewsbury, where they had a brief stop for some lunch at a roadside café. Twenty minutes later they were speeding northwards towards Stoke-on-Trent, where they were able to join the newly-opened M6 motorway, which allowed them to drive even faster. Somewhere around Preston, Johnny asked Annie, his mother-in-law, for the address of their hotel on Morecambe Bay.

She replied, 'Half a mo, I've got it in my handbag! Just a minute while I find it for you!' Minutes passed as the big car sped silently along the motorway.

Suddenly she said in quiet tones, 'I'm sorry, Johnny, but I can't find it anywhere. Do you have it with you, Gwen?'

'Not I, Annie *fach*. I left all the arrangements to you, remember.'

'Damn it all,' Annie muttered. 'I can't think where it could be or what I did with it!'

Johnny, concentrating on his driving, was only half listening to what was going on in the back seat, but whatever it was, it didn't sound good. He sucked in a deep breath before he said tersely, 'Well, ladies, it's a bit too late to find that out now, innit?'

'Well, I can only think that I 'ave left it on the kitchen table. That's where the hotel details must be!'

Johnny sighed and looked towards his wife and shrugged as he said, 'Well, don't worry about it now. We'll sort something out when we get there, okay?' He drove on in silence while he thought about ways to locate the hotel. 'Um, this hotel, is it on the front facing the bay?'

'Oh yes,' his mother in law replied quickly. 'It's right on the front and we had a lovely view of the sea from our window right above the front door.'

Johnny nodded as he looked again at his wife. 'Well, that's something, anyway.' As neither he nor his wife had ever been to Morecambe Bay before, he had no idea, at that moment, what trials and tribulations they would encounter when they arrived at their destination.

About two hours later he found a parking spot on the seafront of Morecambe Bay. He got out of the car to stretch his legs and looked around him. His jaw dropped when he realised that as far as the eye could see there were miles and miles of hotels and boarding houses that were almost identical in shape and size. He looked back down the road they had come in on and noticed a telephone kiosk not too far away. He got back in the car and they all sat in silence as Johnny tried to think of an easy way out of their predicament. He turned in his seat and asked his mother-in-law and Aunty Gwen if they could see anything that looked familiar to them. They both looked out of the car window and slowly shook their heads. Then Aunty Gwen said, 'I remember there was a nice fish and chip shop by the hotel!'

'Ah, but that was right behind the hotel, Gwen, remember?'

'Oh, aye. It was too. I remember our hotel had a big wide curved front step. It was just two steps up to the front door, which was painted green, and it had a big brass knocker and some nice floral curtains. I can remember that much and it was called Sea something.'

Johnny said nothing but pulled a face to Jane as he turned to face the front of the car.

His wife, not having said a word, cleared her throat and said, 'Okay! If this booking has been made by Maggie Williams, there must be some way to get in touch with her to find out the name of the hotel, right?'

'Oh, yes,' came the prompt reply from her mother.

'Not if she's on the same bluddy trip as us, mind!' Gwen said with a serious expression on her round features. 'I'm only saying, that's all!'

'Okay! Let's think a minute. She lives next door but one to the Prince of Wales in Harris street in Waun-gron, right?'

They both nodded agreement to his question.

'Okay, let's see how much change we've got between us and I'll go and speak to the operator at Directory Enquiries to see if I can find a telephone number, and call her house to get some details. If there's anybody there, they should be able to tell us that, isn't it? Time is getting on and we don't want to spend all night sitting by yere in the car, do we?'

Everyone, including his wife gave an emphatic 'No!'

He looked at the handful of small change he had collected and decided that the eight shillings they had between them might not be enough for the long distance calls he anticipated making to Waun-gron in south Wales, and the possibility of some long-winded explanations of their predicament at that particular moment in finding a hotel that was already booked, of which they didn't know the name, or where it was located along this six-mile 'front' of Morecambe Bay.

He put the small change in his jacket pocket and climbed stiffly out of the car, at the same time saying to his passengers, 'So, I'm going across the road to that little shop to get some more change, just in case. I'll be back as quick as I can.'

Crossing the busy road, he entered the little gift shop and asked for a pound's worth of small change for the telephone. The lady behind the counter looked at his with some surprise and said, 'I'm sorry but I can't give you that much change, in case I need it for my customers.'

Johnny frowned and replied. 'I'm in a bit of a pickle and I need to make some long-distance phone calls to south Wales.'

He paused, debating whether to go into explaining the problem facing his family, when she said brightly, 'If you would like to buy something, sir, I would be obliged to provide you with all the change you need to make your phone calls!'

Johnny smiled, relief showing on his face as he thanked her and said, 'I'll have a quarter pound of bonbons and two large bars of Cadbury's Fruit and Nut please, and if I need more change, I'll come back and buy some more.' Handing her a £1 note, he left the shop with all the change he needed.

Returning to the car, he handed his unwanted purchases to Jane and hurried off to the telephone kiosk some 20 yards away. Once inside the box he arranged the coins he thought he would need in rows, pennies at the top and sixpences and shillings below them. He took out his notebook and unscrewed his fountain pen in readiness. Then taking a deep breath, he dialled the number for the long-distance operator.

'Yes, I would like the telephone number for a Mrs Maggie Williams please. She lives in Harris Street in the village of Waun-gron in south Wales, Oh, sorry that's in Glamorgan. Yes, I'll wait, thank you.'

'I'm sorry, sir, but I cannot find any Maggie Williams in Harris Street in that village!'

'Er, what about in any other street, then?'

'I'll check that for you, sir...'

Johnny glanced at his watch and then up at the sky, which seemed to be getting darker by the second.

'Yes, operator! No one by that name then? What about some other Williams, then?'

He waited while she searched. Minutes went by swiftly then she came back to him and said, 'I have checked and rechecked all the Williams in that village – that's about 35 separate Williamses, sir – and found no Maggie or Margaret. I'm sorry, but I can't help you any further with your search.'

'Okay, thank you for your help with this name. Now, could you give me the telephone number of the Prince of Wales pub, Harris Street in the same village, Waun-gron, please?'

After a brief pause, she provided the number requested and then said in pleasant tones, 'Is there anything else I can help you with, sir?'

'No, no, that's perfect, and thank you very much for your help.' He was about to put down the phone and call the Prince of Wales pub when she said, 'I can connect you from here, if you like. All you have to do is put in more coins when the operator tells you.'

'Oh, that would be great, thank you.'

Moments later the phone was answered.

'Hello?' said Johnny. 'Yes, I hope you can help me – I'm looking for a Mrs Maggie Williams, who lives next door but one to your pub. Do you know her?'

'This is Joe Lloyd and I'm the landlord yere and 'ave been for the past five years, and I can tell you now there is no Mrs Maggie Williams living by me. Sorry, mate!'

'But my mother-in-law told me... just a minute, I've got to put more coins in. Yes, she told me that she lives right by there...'

'Listen! I've just told you. I know very well who is living by me and it is not the lady you are asking about.'

'It's definitely not Maggie Williams, then?'

'No! Definitely not!'

The phone went dead in his hand. He stared at it for a full minute until it started beeping, then gathering up all the coins, he returned in an irritated mood to his car. He opened the car door and almost flung himself into the front seat, where he sat in silence for a few seconds.

Jane, sensing his mood, hesitated for a moment and then asked, 'Well? Did you find her number?'

'No! No, I didn't find her bluddy number! To all intents and purposes, she doesn't exist in Waun-gron. I have spent the last ten minutes talking to the operator, who checked every one of the Williamses living in the village and couldn't find her. I even called the Prince of Wales pub and spoke to Joe Lloyd, the landlord, and he said there is no Maggie Williams living by him.'

'Well, of course not!' his mother-in-law called out from the back seat. 'That's because Williams was her name before she married Dai Walters. We never used his name when we spoke about her to anybody because he wasn't from our village, he was from away somewhere. As I said before, we have known her since we were children in school together so we always called her Maggie Williams. Then after, when Dai Walters died and she was a widow, there was no need to use her married name, was there? She'll always be Maggie Williams to us, won't she, Gwen?'

'Well, yes!' her sister replied, nodding her head in agreement.

Stunned at this seemingly simple revelation, Johnny stared open-mouthed at his wife, who reached out and, gently squeezing his arm, smiled and shrugged her shoulders.

He took a deep breath and slowly got out of the car to stand in the fresh breeze off the sea as his annoyance abated. He went back to the telephone kiosk and dialled the number for the Prince of Wales pub.

Moments later the familiar voice of the landlord boomed out of the receiver. 'Prince of Wales!'

'Oh, hello. It's me again! Sorry, but I have just been informed that Maggie Williams' married name is Walters. She's Maggie Walters!'

'Aye, aye! That's right! She's a widow and I don't have to send for anyone to speak with you. Here's her phone number off the top of my head and her daughter should be home at this time of the evening, so she can help you. Good luck, mate!'

A few minutes later, Johnny returned to his car in high spirits, laughing as he opened the car door, saying, 'I've got the address of your hotel, ladies! It is called the Sea View Hotel and it's about halfway along the front at the fifth set of traffic lights from where we are. I've had a quick look and it's not far away, so let's get going, is it?'

CHAPTER 28

Wetting the Baby's Head

JOHNNY AND ALAN entered the Plough Inn one Wednesday evening. As Johnny pushed open the heavy oak door into the bar, they were met with the loud clamour of raised voices from a crowd of early drinkers, who appeared to be well into their cups. Johnny glanced at his watch and noted that it was almost 7.30. He looked at Alan, who shrugged as they eased their way through the crowd standing in the middle of the room. Arriving at their usual spot at the far end of the long bar, they saw Trefor pulling pints just as fast as he could manage and lining them up along the bar. He looked up with a grin. Alan raised his eyebrows and asked, 'Has this lot been yere all day, Tref?'

'No, by damn! They all came in yere together right on 6 o'clock as I opened the front door.'

Johnny turned to survey the crowd at the other end of the long room and noticed there were quite a number of strangers amongst the usual Plough customers. 'So, what's this all about then, Tref?'

Trefor straightened up and wiped a trace of perspiration from his brow. 'Yes, Johnny, you might well ask. Tommy Price's daughter has just presented him with his first grandson and he got this crowd together to wet the baby's head. You know how that works, don't you? He's put £100 over the bar for as much beer as I can serve until it's gone. To tell you the truth, I've lost count already because I was pulling so many pints to get them started. Yere, you two might as well have a pint each and go over there to him and thank him at the same time as...'

'Congratulating him!' Johnny cut in to finish the sentence.

Alan took a good swig from his pint and looked across the room at the crowd around the large table. 'Well, Trefor, I would have a hard time believing that this lot had only been drinking in yere for less than two hours, if you hadn't told me.'

'That's what an open bar and free beer will do for you,' Trefor replied, grinning broadly.

'What a bluddy row they're making, though. It's enough to deafen you. Some of them don't look as though they can handle more than a pint or two at best!'

'Oh, this is nothing compared to the row old Fred caused in yere one night a few years back. That was about wetting the baby's head, too.'

'Aye? Well, go on then, Tref.' Johnny nudged Alan and grinned.

'Well, let me think about it for a minute to get the story straight, is it? Yes, well, it was busy in yere one Saturday night and in comes a crowd from Penderyn and a couple of boys from Ystradfellte. Naturally everybody had had a few pints by this time and one of the boys from Penderyn happened to mention that his daughter had given birth to a baby boy just the other week. Of course, Fred was listening to this and he wanted to know who they were talking about. Well, one of them stood up and shouted above the noise that it was his grandson and the little one's father was Tommy Phillips.

'"I know him!" Fred shouted back above the noise. "I was there to wet the baby's head in The Lamb in Penderyn."

'"I don't bluddy think so, Fred. You were nowhere near the place cos I knew everyone who was in that room."

'"Aye, I was," he shouted back. "Listen! I've been to every one of the new babies born around yere, right!"

'Fred was shouting from his seat near Old John Shinkins on the settle over there and the other boys were at this end sitting around a table by the dartboard, right behind you over there. Well, there was a place. I know I always like to have a row in yere, but this was going beyond. Then one of the boys stood up and shouted, "Hey, Fred! What about the baby that was born to the daughter of the Pant Farm, then?"

'"Aye, aye. I was in the New Inn in Ystradfellte for that one. It was a little girl, wasn't it? I remember it like it was yesterday, boys. Price, that was her name – Annie May Price, and her husband is John Price and he's from Aberaman, down by Aberdare."

'"Okay, Fred, I'll give you that one. What about the grandson born into the Davies family at Carreg Fawr, then?"

'"Aye, I was in the New Inn for that one too," said Fred. "I remember he was a bompah. When he was born, he weighed 10 ½ lb – that's almost grown up. C'mon, boys, every one you ask about, I was there. I even know who was born in Llwyn Onn, and up by the Red Lion, and Mrs Watkins in the Red Lion always gives me a free pint when I go in there because I get everyone singing when there's a do to wet the baby's head. Boys, you can't tell me anything about any babies being born around yere because Fred was there, right!"

'Then one of the boys from Ystradfellte asked Fred about the baby that was born about two weeks before belonging to the Castell Farm on the road to Sennybridge.'

'"Aye, aye! I remember that one too. I was on the bluddy farm when she was confined and we all went down to the New Inn for a few drinks."

'"Wait on, Fred! Wait a bluddy minute! No, you didn't! I was helping out on that farm with the shearing because they had a load of sheep. She was never confined at home because they sent her by ambulance to a hospital in Merthyr."

'Fred stood in the middle of the room, his pint inches from his lips, and shouted, "What are you bothering about? I was there, mun!"

'"Not this one, Fred! You are saying lies. She was in Merthyr hospital. I've got you on this one."

'Fred took a swig from his pint and said, "Well, I can't be every-bluddy-where, can I?"

'After that it went a bit quieter because Fred went into the front room and began to bother some of my customers with his old stories so I went in there and spoke to him in Welsh: "Fred, *mae angen i mi siarad â chi*," so he came out and I told him off again for bothering people and he went back into the bar and was quiet for the rest of the night.'

'That's hard to believe, Tref.'

'Aye, I agree, but it's right enough what I'm telling you. The noise yere tonight is nothing. I have a question for you, boys, me being a bachelor: how old is a baby before it starts to walk?'

Alan shrugged. 'I don't know for sure but I think it's about nine months.'

Johnny, straight-faced, said, 'I was three years old before I started to walk.'

Alan turned to face him. 'How's that, then? Was there something wrong with your legs?'

'Nah! Everybody said I was so handsome as a baby, nobody wanted to put me down!'

CHAPTER 29

On Being
Sent to Coventry

THE MOMENT ALAN and Johnny entered the Plough Inn, Trefor began waving his arms to attract their attention.

'Hey, Alan! I need to ask you something. Come over by yere a minute!'

Johnny looked sideways at his brother-in-law and asked, 'What in the world have you done now, *brawd*?'

'I dunno, do I? Yes, Trefor: how can I help you, sir?'

Trefor, his round features creasing into a broad smile, replied, 'Well, Alan. Listen. You work on the opencast site, don't you?'

'Yes, I do, Tref – but which one are you talking about? There are a few in this area, mind.'

'Oh! Oh, I think it's the one over by Banwen mountain. A chap came in yere this afternoon with a funny story about one of their lorry drivers, but he was laughing so much when he was telling the story, I could barely understand what he was trying to tell us. Do you happen to know? Have you yerd anything funny about one of your drivers?'

Alan grinned and winked at Johnny. 'Yes, Tref, as a matter of fact I have – but before I say anything, two pints of best bitter, if you please.'

Trefor's jaw fell open with surprise, then he laughed and replied, 'Yes, sir, Alan! Right away, Alan!'

Alan took a long swig from his pint and smacked his lips with satisfaction. 'Damn, this is a great pint, Trefor.'

'Yes, yes, I know that!' he said testily. 'Now, will you get on with the story about your lorry driver? I've been on pins waiting for you to come in, mun!'

Alan turned to face the other end of the bar and called out. 'Boys! Come down yere a minute and listen to this. It's a gem!'

The usual suspects around the card table rose as one and crowded around Alan and Johnny. Alan cleared his throat and with a slight bow to everyone he said, 'In my capacity as a site foreman I have made it my business...'

'Aww, come off it, Alan,' Trefor interrupted. 'Be serious for once, mun, and tell us what happened!'

'Aye, okay. Tommy John, one of our lorry drivers, he's been working on the site since it first opened. Well, he was called to the site office a few days ago and he told me that he thought he was going to get the sack because he was the oldest driver there. He'd yerd somewhere that older drivers who had never had an accident were overdue for one and that worried him no end. However, instead of being given his marching orders, he was told he had to go and take delivery of a brand new 18-wheeler from the factory in Coventry. He told me this was a bit of a shock because he had never driven anything outside the local area. In fact, he said he had never driven anything as far as Swansea or Cardiff! Anyway, Bob, our office manager, handed him a voucher for the one-way railway journey to Coventry via Birmingham. He then gave him the address of the factory where he was to collect the new lorry and £75 in cash to pay for his overnight stay in Coventry.

Well, poor Tommy said he didn't know what to say and he thought if he refused, he might get sacked on the spot. So he put everything into a big buff envelope and went home to pack a few things he thought he might need, and caught the Red and White bus down to Neath. He gave the man at the ticket office his travel voucher and was told the train would be there in about 20 minutes and he would have to change at Cardiff and Birmingham. He told me that changing trains at Cardiff was no problem but when he got to Birmingham, he had to ask directions and he said he had no idea what they were saying. He told me it all sounded like a foreign language to him. Eventually he arrived in Coventry and had much the same difficulty in understanding what people said to him.'

'So, he was a poor Welshman lost among the English heathens, then,' Bobby chipped in with a grin.

'Aye, aye. Something like that. Anyway, he stayed in the Railway Hotel and said he had hardly a wink of sleep, worrying about finding the factory in the morning. He told me he went to ask a taxi driver and showed him the address where he had to go and asked how far away it was. The driver said it was only about 20 minutes away and it would cost about five quid. He said this chap told him, "I'll take you there right away," so he jumped into the cab and next thing he was at the factory gate.

'He said he was very relieved to be where he was supposed to be. He paid the driver and walked over to the gate office. There he showed his collection invoice to the security guard and was told to wait while the guard phoned for someone to help him. Minutes later a young woman waved for him to follow her through a maze of passages until suddenly he was back in the fresh air, where row after row of 18-wheelers stood silently, waiting for drivers like him to bring them to life.

'He said this young girl took his arm and guided him towards a small cabin at the edge of the parking area. The man inside held his hand out for the paperwork, glanced through it and said, "Just sign here, mate, and she's all yours. Here's a local road map for you to find your way sort of south-west. From there it should be quite easy to find your way back to south Wales. They've got good roads down that way now. Best of luck, mate!"

'He told me that he sat in the cab of that brand new lorry for ages, pretending to look at all the unfamiliar controls, until the chap from the cabin came over and wanted to know if everything was okay. So, he started it up and drove it slowly out of the factory yard and onto the main road – and that's where his problems started.

'Somehow, he missed his turn-off in the rush-hour traffic. He told me that he'd never seen so many vehicles on the road in one place at the same time before. He said he thought he saw the road he was supposed to be on but then found he was lost *and* driving an unfamiliar vehicle. It was then, he told me, that he began driving this 18-wheeler round and round this housing estate looking for his way back to the road he'd been on, but he somehow kept missing his turn off. At that point he spotted a policeman standing on the corner, and he stopped to ask him directions on how to get on the road for south Wales. The policeman said it was not a problem and gave him a scribbled map to guide him.

'Then, as he handed over the scrap of paper, the policeman said, "It should be pretty easy for you from here – I just saw a fleet of your lorries going that way about five minutes ago."

'Tommy said he didn't like to tell the officer that it was Tommy he'd seen, going round and round the housing estate!'

Trefor and all the others listening to Alan's story broke up into laughter at the end of his tale.

CHAPTER 30

Mishap in the *Glowty*

IT WAS EARLY May and most of the farmers in the district were preparing for shearing their flocks. Each one had their farmhands searching the fields and hills on foot and on horseback for any stray sheep, with dogs to round them all up, before the warm weather came in.

Johnny, as usual, was standing talking to Trefor at the far end of the bar when Twm came up for a refill and asked him, 'Where's your shadow, then?'

'*Shomai*, Twm! At this very moment, I've got no idea.' Johnny glanced at his watch. 'He's probably soaking in his bath after a long day on the opencast site. Why do you ask?'

Twm stroked his beard. 'Well…' he paused, 'I'm planning on having my sheep sheared next weekend, if the weather comes good. I'll need a few "volunteers" to help out and I wondered...'

Johnny glanced at him while in his mind he looked ahead for any plans he might have made. 'Could be okay for me, Twm. Next weekend is a bank holiday and I never go anywhere on a bank holiday. Too many idiot drivers on the road for my liking! At the moment, as far as I can see ahead, I can be there to help out. It's not at Tai Cwpla, is it?'

'Thanks, Johnny. No, it's at my other place, where you go to pick mushrooms. Didn't think I knew that, did you?' He laughed at the surprised look on Johnny's face.

'Right! How many ewes have you got over there then?'

'Oh, about 700 at the last count, and that's without counting this year's lambs.'

'And you expect to get them all sheared in one day?'

'Oh, aye. I've got three of the best shearers around yere coming to my place. They're not cheap, mind, but it pays to have them boys in the long run. It means I'll have my fleeces ready to sell before anyone else, so I can get top price for them.'

'Well, that makes a lot of sense.'

'Of course it does! So, I can count on you for bank holiday Monday, then?'

'Well, yes. Are there any other boys going to help you from around yere? I'll have room in my car for a few.'

'Aye, aye. I think I'll have a few of the boys who usually help us farmers out. I'll have to let you know later, okay?'

'No problem, Twm.' Johnny picked up his pint as Twm returned to the card table.

On the following Sunday morning, Johnny was having his usual pre-lunch pint when Twm turned around in his chair at the card table. 'Hey, Johnny! Are you still okay for tomorrow morning?'

'Well, yes! I told you yes before, mun!'

'Aye, I know! The old memory sometimes plays tricks,' Twm laughed. 'Okay, then, can you be by Siop John in the morning by about 6.30?'

'Aye, okay. I've got room for three, mind.'

'Right you are, then. There'll be Danny Thomas, Tomos, and perhaps Bobby. He's not sure yet.'

'Aye, okay, Twm. No problem.' Johnny finished his pint and left the bar.

At 6.30 he parked outside Siop John, switched off the engine and closed his eyes. He was startled by a sharp rap on the roof and saw the smiling face of Danny Thomas almost pressed flat against his side window. He unlocked the doors and his three passengers piled in. Twenty minutes later he drove slowly down into the farmyard at Hepste Fawr.

Twm, all smiles, was there to greet them as they climbed out of the car.

'Right, boys! Yere we go. You Danny: you look after the ewes inside the *glowty*, as you've done before. I've got a small piece fenced off, with a door to the field where most of my flock is penned.' Danny nodded and headed off in the direction of the old cowshed.

'Bobby and Tomos will bring more ewes in as the ones inside are sheared and turned loose. Your job, Johnny, is to catch each ewe and carry it over to the shearers as they need one.' He laughed. 'Today we're going to make good use of your broad shoulders. What you have to do is this.' He stepped into the pen and grabbed a good handful of fleece on each side of the sheep and lifted the animal off the ground, then turned and walked with it to the nearest shearer to place its back end on the ground in front of him. The shearer bent forward, straddled the ewe, and held it in a firm grip across its neck and breastbone. At the same time, he began shearing with his wide-bladed electric machine. Down the neck and across the front, then down each flank. The wool peeled away with ease while Twm looked on with satisfaction at the speed with which it was completed.

'Right, then, Johnny! Do you think you can handle that?'

'No doubt at all, Twm. Let's get going, then.'

At about ten o'clock, Twm called a halt for everyone to have a fifteen-minute break.

'How are you feeling there, Johnny? You're keeping up well with the shearers.'

'Aye, not bad at all, Twm. Good thing my normal job is in a piecework shop so I'm used to chasing the clock and doing repetitive work. I just had to make a few adjustments, but I'm okay, thank you.'

'Aye, aye,' Danny chipped in. 'It didn't take 'im long, Twm.'

It was about an hour or so after they'd taken a break for dinner that things went a bit haywire. The three shearers had set up their positions at the back of the *glowty*. When each ewe was shorn, they just let them go. Sensing freedom and seeing the open door, the ewes bolted for the light like Olympic sprinters. Some of them bounded though the air on stiff legs, like lambs in spring but weighing a lot more.

At a certain point, Johnny had just grabbed another ewe and was in the act of turning to pass it to a shearer when one of the ewes which had just been released leapt right into his face. Instinctively, he grabbed whatever it was that had hit him and held it by the neck up against the wall. In an instant, his cheek and eye seemed to explode with pain and flashes of light shot back and forth across his brain.

'Bluddy 'ell boys! What was that? What the 'ell happened?'

'Put that bluddy sheep down, Johnny! That's the one that just jumped into your face, mun!' Danny shouted. 'Twm, come and look at this!'

Twm arrived at a run and tried his best not to laugh at the sight of Johnny's rapidly swelling face. He put his arm around Johnny's shoulders and led him slowly outside to where ice-cold water was coming from the spring that fed a large galvanised trough beside the *glowty*.

'You need to bathe that eye with cold water, Johnny. It's almost closed already. Damn it all, you had a nasty knock there.'

'Yes, Twm – I can bluddy feel that!' Johnny delved in his pocket for a handkerchief. Folding it, he soaked it in the running water and gently pressed it against the throbbing pain. He wasn't sure if it was the ice-cold water that accelerated the situation, but in an instant he was unable to see out of his left eye at all.

Old Owen, one of Twm's neighbours, who had seen the damage, came over to take a closer look and gently held Johnny's face in his gnarled hands. 'Well, this is going to be a beautiful black eye. When I was doing a bit of boxing and they saw an eye like this, they got a piece of steak and put it on there to reduce the swelling.'

Twm, listening in, said, 'Sorry, Johnny, I don't have any steak to give you. Listen, I think you'd better go home, if you can still drive, and take a spell with that eye. There's not a lot left to do and you've done a 'ell of a job for me, and I thank you for that. We'll manage the rest and I 'spect I'll see you in the Plough later in the week. Thanks again, mun.'

Johnny just nodded, waved to the others and drove slowly and carefully out of the farmyard.

When he got home, the first thing he did was to take a couple of aspirin and a few cups of water, then opened the fridge to get some ice – and spotted a plate of steak. He thought immediately about the remedy that Old Owen had suggested. He took the plate and walked to the window where the light was better, and looked at the steaks arranged neatly on the plate. He chose the smallest and thickest and, after putting the plate back in the fridge, lay down on the settee with the slab of meat resting on his damaged eye and cheekbone. He had no idea how long he lay there before his wife came home from her mother's and raised her voice to ask him, 'Johnny! What the heck are you doing with that piece of silverside steak on your face? Are you mad or what? No, wait a minute, somebody gave you a biff! Is that it?'

'Now, how likely is that?' He sat up and took the steak off his face. 'This is not a good time to start a row, is it?'

His wife looked at the mess on his face and decided this was not a good time to laugh either. Instead she said, pointing to the steak. 'Well, you've used that bit now so that's your share. Do you know just how expensive that cut of meat is? And just look at you, Johnny, you haven't even washed. Oh, what am I going to do with you?'

Johnny held his head in his hands. 'Don't bother me for a minute, will you? My head is thumping like a bluddy trip hammer!'

Later she said, 'That eye looks really bad. I think you should go and see Dr Evans in the morning – and wear some dark glasses when you go.'

'Aye, okay. Listen, I've got to pop over to the Plough for a minute…'

'Aye? Now that's a likely story, isn't it? You going to the Plough for a minute.'

'No, no. It's right enough. They will be telling all sorts of stories about this.' He touched his face and winced.

He entered the bar in the Plough to cheers from the regulars, just as Danny Thomas was describing what had happened.

'Aye, boys, you should have seen. This bluddy ewe was coming across the floor full tilt just as Johnny turned. He didn't have a chance as it jumped right into 'is face, but I'll tell you this for nothing: he didn't go down, no, by damn. He didn't go down. That shows just how tough that man is!'

Johnny, standing just inside the room, tried to grin and said, 'Thank you, Danny, for those few kind words. I'll see you boys later in the week, okay.'

The day after the bank holiday, Johnny reported for work as usual and informed his foreman that he needed to see his doctor. He didn't need to explain: it was fairly obvious why. In the surgery, he sat waiting patiently, trying to think of a reasonable excuse for his visit. In the end he decided that the truth of what had happened was the only option.

He sat in front of Dr Evans and slowly removed his dark glasses. Dr Evans took one look and burst out laughing. Finally, between fits of laughing, he asked politely, 'So, what exactly happened and what does the other bloke look like?'

'As a matter of fact, doctor, it was nothing like that at all.' Johnny paused and took in a deep breath and said as casually as possible, 'I got headbutted by a bluddy sheep...'

Dr Evans burst out laughing, holding his sides as if in pain. 'Oh *Duw*, Johnny, you're priceless. Tell me exactly what happened, please.'

Johnny sniffed and let out a deep sigh. 'I was helping out with the shearing on one of the local farms and as I turned around, this sheep which had just been sheared jumped in the air and butted me in the face.' He paused and said with a slight grin, 'I don't think it was intentional, mind.'

Dr Evans once again broke down at Johnny's innocent-sounding remark, laughing until tears ran down his cheeks.

'Johnny, I think you had better go down to the hospital and have an X-ray taken. It's possible that the blow you've taken on your cheek could have damaged the bone. Take this note with you and bring the X-ray back to me and I'll see you later.' He reached out and shook Johnny by the hand. 'Thank you for making my day, Johnny.'

Later in the day, Dr Evans pronounced that indeed Johnny's cheekbone was cracked and he thought that some nerve damage had occurred to that part of his face. His advice was to take it easy and it would repair itself in due course.

That night in the Plough, everyone agreed that the range of colours around Johnny's eye far exceeded the black eye Trefor had got from Ned Pant-y-waun's punch, and could be a stiff challenger to the many coloured patches on Trefor's old woollen jersey.

Epilogue

I AM SURE the stories of Fred and his antics will continue to surface in the Rhyd-y-Groes area for many years to come and his son Colin will no doubt have fun relating some of his more memorable escapades, but for now, that is enough.

The Plough Inn will remain the centre of interest for the landlord, Trefor 'Plough' Williams, as he approaches retirement.

The butcher will no doubt continue his relentless badgering of Trefor Plough as long as he believes his early morning phone calls are annoying him.

The two councillors, Alan George and Johnny Wills, will continue to strive for ways to improve life for the people of the village they grew up in, with all the power they can muster.

Sadly, some of the real-life characters included in this story have now departed this life for greener pastures. But the village? It will survive and continue to prosper, as it has done since time immemorial.

Glossary
of local terms

Arglwydd Mawr (Welsh)	Good Lord!
bach (Welsh)	small, or an affectionate term
bit simple	not all there, vague
bois bach! (Welsh)	good grief!, damn
bompah	whopper
Bore da (Welsh)	Good morning
brawd (Welsh)	brother
brembutter	bread and butter
butty	mate/friend at work or play
by yere	by here (= here)
byth (Welsh)	ever/never
caib (Welsh)	pick
chopsin'	gossiping
cleckabox	chatterbox, gossip
clecs (Welsh)	gossip, rumours
(in) clink	(in) prison

cwtch	to hide, huddle or to cuddle (only the Welsh know how to cwtch!) – also used as a name for the cupboard under the stairs.
der	yes/well now!
Diolch (yn fawr iawn) (Welsh)	Thank you (very much)
dipstick	stupid person
Duw (Welsh)	God
flush	with money
fr'ages	for ages
glowty (Welsh)	cowshed
(all) gone out	taken aback, surprised, shocked
haisht!	be quiet!
half a pint a corner	small wager on a game of cribbage
iawn (Welsh)	OK
in your cups	drunk
innit?	isn't it?
Mae angen i mi siarad â chi (Welsh)	I need to talk to you
mandrel	a small miner's coal pick
mun	man/fellow/mate
(in) the nick	(in) prison
no light on top	a bit simple minded
now in a minute	later
now jest	a short time before

(be) off top	mad as hell
(be) 'off' with	to be angry with
on pins	on tenterhooks
open tap	beginning of beer being allowed to be served
Paid sôn! (Welsh)	Don't bring that up!/You don't say!
Peidiwch sôn! (Welsh)	as *Paid sôn!*, but to someone you don't know well or to more than one person
pilk	small, skinny person; a lightweight
pop	fizzy drink, e.g. lemonade
potch	bother
(had a bit of a) pull	(had some kind of) injury or illness
shomai (Welsh)	hello (regional version of *shwmae*)
skelp it	scarper, get away as quick as you can
(have/take a) spell	(have/take a) break or short rest
strap	credit
tad-cu (Welsh)	grandfather, granddad
tampin'	furious
tanner	a pre-decimal sixpenny piece
The tears ran down my legs.	I wet myself laughing.
There was a place.	What a mess!/What a commotion!/What a row!

tidy	good
Tower, the	Tower Colliery
twp (Welsh)	stupid
twpsyn (Welsh)	stupid person
twtti down	crouch/squat/bend down
waun (Welsh)	moor or meadow
yerd	heard
yere	here
yuge	huge

Also from Y Lolfa:

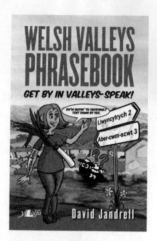

£3.99

Humorous guide to Valleys-speak, affectionately
poking fun at the everyday language of the Valleys.

£3.95

Light-hearted look at the humour and
idiosyncrasies of some stock Valleys characters.

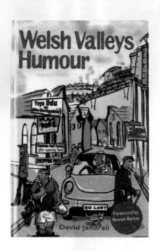

£3.95

£3.95

Two tongue-in-cheek guides to the unique dialect
and humour of the Valleys – foreword by Ronnie Barker.